TWO OF A KIND

Two of a Kind

Suzanne Zuckerman

a heavenly Romance

Published by E.P. Dutton, Inc., New York

TWO OF A KIND

Copyright © 1982 by Suzanne Zuckerman

ISBN: 0-525-66806-3

A Heavenly Romance, published by
E.P. Dutton, Inc., 2 Park Ave., New York, N.Y. 10016

Editor: Kathy O'Hehir

Cover Photographer: Ira Finke

10 9 8 7 6 5 4 3 2 1

Printed in the U.S.A.

chapter

"Carolyn Lenore Clark, what is the matter with you?" her mother's voice shook. She moved the clothing around the dressing room.

"Nothing's the matter," replied Carol. "I just don't see anything I like."

"What about this blue dress with the Peter Pan collar? It matches your eyes. It's adorable."

"I'm going to high school, not kindergarten!" exclaimed Carol.

"I know that, dear, but do you know what you want?"

Carol knew her mother's tone meant trouble. "Let's go home," she suggested.

"We are not leaving this store until you choose two outfits. We won't have time for shopping after you start high school."

"All right, I'll take the blue dress and the red plaid skirt."

"Good," her mother smiled. "That skirt goes with the ruffled blouse."

"No!" Carol felt like she might cry. "I don't want any more ruffles. I'm tired of looking cute."

"Darling," Mrs. Clark sat on the pink satin chair, "high school's the time to look your best."

"Why does my best have to be cute?"

"Carol, you have lovely coloring. You have naturally curly hair. And you are petite."

Carol held the blue dress against her body. The soft wool felt good. The triple mirrors reflected her differing front and back. They also showed her mother's impatient smile.

"You see how nice it looks," insisted Mrs. Clark. "The Havor girls would give anything for a figure like yours."

"If they gave up sugar, they'd be fine," snapped Carol. Her own anger surprised her. "At least they're not short," she added softly.

"You're not short," responded her mother. "Five feet is a perfectly normal height for a woman."

Carol held up the tartan skirt.

"I think you're tired," she concluded. "Choose a blouse and we'll go home."

"All right, you take these to the cashier and I'll join you in a minute." Carol handed her mother several packages of tights and leotards.

"These things are so expensive. And they do nothing for you. Are you sure you need this many?" asked Mrs. Clark.

"The high school handbook suggested two leotards for dance class," Carol replied. "And tights are warmer than stockings or knee socks."

"You could have at least chosen some bright colors."

"I'm tired of bright colors." Carol declared as she left the dressing room.

"I'll meet you at the desk," agreed her mother with a sigh. She picked up the blue dress, the red skirt, and the ruffled blouse. "Don't take too long," Mrs. Clark called to her daughter as she tucked the blouse between the other clothing.

Carol arrived at the cashier with three turtleneck shirts in black, navy, and forest green.

"Is that what you really want?"

"Yes!"

At home in her pink and white room, Carol unpacked her shopping bags.

"Oh, Mother, you didn't!" she yelled.

"Oh, Carol, I did!" called Mrs. Clark from the kitchen. "You'll be glad to have that pretty blouse once school starts!"

Carol left the tags on the blouse. She hung it behind all the other ruffled blouses in her closet. She carefully removed the tights and leotards from their plastic packages. As she folded them into her underwear drawer, Carol thought about choosing dance instead of hockey for gym. An actress should know how to dance, she concluded.

High school's going to be wonderful, she told herself. They won't treat me like a child just because I'm small. She smiled with pleasure remembering the class program she'd chosen: dance, history, English, French, drama, mathematics. Her parents had insisted on the mathematics.

In elementary and junior high school there had been no choices. Everyone took the same exact program. If she'd gone to East Egelton High, there would have been no choice, either. When the county rearranged the school districts, Carol's mother was very upset. She tried to convince the family to move. But Carol insisted on attending the newer school. She had never felt comfortable with the snobby, rich kids from Crown Point.

"Carol, come down and set the table," her mother yelled.

"I'm putting everything away," Carol returned.

"Hurry up, your father will be home any minute."

Carol finished hanging up the blue dress and the red plaid skirt. She put the turtlenecks on a shelf, and she took the boxes, bags, and tissue paper downstairs.

3

"Put that mess with the garbage outside; then set the table."

"I'll be right in," Carol replied.

Outside in the yard Carol took a deep breath. Fall is the nicest time in Connecticut, she thought. Their giant maple had just begun to change color. A yellow leaf edged in red drifted slowly down.

"How's my little Sarah Bernhardt?" called her father. He walked toward her along the driveway.

"I'm not little; tomorrow I start high school," Carol yelled back.

"So you do; so you do," he repeated as he bent to kiss her cheek. "It all goes so fast," he muttered to himself.

"Don, is that you?" his wife shouted through the screened dining room window.

"Yes, dear, I'm home," he replied, "I'll be right in."

"Tell Carol to set the table," added Mrs. Clark.

"You heard," he smiled at his daughter. "What are you doing out here?"

"I was throwing away some wrappings. Mom bought me new clothes for school."

"A high-school student has to dress right," he teased. Mr. Clark held the aluminum door for Carol.

"I hear there's a fashion show after dinner," Mr. Clark announced to his wife as he kissed her.

"Yes," she replied, "that's a good idea. You tell Carol how cu..." she paused, "how sweet she looks in her new clothes."

"Sweet's worse than cute," complained Carol as she took the clean plates from the dishwasher.

Carol finished folding the paper napkins, but before she could put them under the forks, the phone rang.

"You answer it, Carol, please," called her mother

4

from the kitchen. "And tell Mary-Lu we're just sitting down to supper."

"Mom, that's not fair. You don't know it's Mary-Lu," she replied, rushing for the den extension.

"Hello, may I help you?" intoned Carol in her most adult manner.

"Hello yourself, what's up?"

"I was expecting someone else."

"You'll just have to settle for plain old me," responded Mary-Lu. "Is your someone else taking you out tonight?"

"No, tomorrow's school," Carol exclaimed.

"Good! You can meet me at the corner of Maple and North Road. I'm sneaking out right after dinner."

"Are you grounded again?"

"What do you mean, 'again'? I'm always grounded. If they could they'd lock me up and throw away the key."

"Carol, dinner now! Say goodbye to Mary-Lu."

"Mom's calling me."

"I can hear her," said Mary-Lu.

"I'll be right there, Mom," yelled Carol.

"Do you have to shout in my ear?"

"I'm sorry."

"Good, now you owe me one. I'll see you at North and Maple right after dinner."

"I can't."

"You can! It'll still be light. Just tell them you're meeting me for an hour."

"Carol, come in here now!"

"Just for an hour?"

"Ah, come on, Carol; it's your last night of freedom."

"Carol, supper's getting cold!"

"I've got to go, I'll see you later."

"Good!" The receiver clicked off in Carol's ear.

I didn't mean that, thought Carol as she hurried into the dining room.

"What's happening to Mary-Lu?" asked Mr. Clark.

Carol seated herself and unfolded her napkin. "She wants me to meet her after dinner. She says it's my last night of freedom."

"Is that how you feel?" asked her father, passing the salad.

"No, I think high school's going to be wonderful," answered Carol.

"Mary-Lu's not much of a student," commented Mrs. Clark.

"She could be if she stopped running after boys all the time," Carol defended her friend.

"I wouldn't bet my dessert on that," teased her father as her mother began to clear the table.

"I wish she were going to West High with me."

"You'll meet lots of new friends," Mr. Clark reassured his daughter.

"I suppose so," she replied, carrying her plate into the kitchen. "It's just that I'd like to know someone there before I go."

"You do," answered her mother. "David White goes to West High."

"Dr. White's son?" asked Carol. "He's too old. I mean, he's a senior. He probably wouldn't even remember me." Carol felt surprised at the way her words tumbled over each other.

"Nonsense," responded Mrs. Clark, "he'd probably be delighted to show you around. I'll phone his mother right after we do the dishes."

Carol half choked on her milk. "You don't have to do that. I'll be fine. Besides, I'm supposed to meet Mary-Lu."

"Tell you what," said her father, "I'll do the dishes

6

tonight. You and Mary-Lu enjoy your last night of freedom."

"Thanks, Dad . . ."

Mrs. Clark cut in, "I expect you back by eight at the latest. You two are not to go biking around in the dark."

"Yes, Mom; thanks Dad; see you later," answered Carol as she ran toward the door.

"Thank goodness you're early," Mary-Lu greeted her friend. "Come on, hurry, we're stashing our bikes in Joe's garage."

"What?" replied Carol.

"I told you, it's our last night of freedom! We've got dates with Micky and Joe at the Corner Place."

"That's a bar. We can't go in there."

"They never check ID; look, if you're nervous, I'll give you my swim club card. Micky fixed it up. It says I'm legal. Besides, all I ever have is a cola or two."

"You've been there before?"

"Just a couple of times."

"Well, I don't think I want to go there, Mary-Lu," replied Carol.

"What will I tell the guys? They're expecting you."

"You should have asked me!"

"Would you have come if I asked? Stop being silly. It's fun. They have a great juke box and lots of video games."

"Mom wants me back before dark."

"You're not a baby anymore."

"That's not the problem," insisted Carol. "I wanted to spend the evening with you."

"If you want to be with me, come to the Corner."

"No, I don't want to go to a bar, and I don't want to be with Joe and Micky, either."

"If you don't want to be with them, you don't want

7

to be with me! Bye, Carol." Mary-Lu wheeled her bike up the gravel drive. "Have a good time at West High."

Carol rode slowly toward home. She circled the nearby blocks until eight.

chapter

★₊★ 2 ★₊★

Carol walked through the cool September morning to catch the bus. The bright sun reflected on the jewel-colored leaves. She wanted to kick at the drifting piles that lined the streets, but Carol feared ruining her new black tights. She wore the tartan skirt, the black turtle-neck, and a heavy, red wool cardigan.

The combination distressed her mother. "You can't play Plain Jane on the first day of school," Mrs. Clark said glumly. Carol refused to change. No more little girl look, she thought triumphantly. But now, as she walked alone toward the chattering crowd at the bus stop, Carol felt unsure. Perhaps her mother was right and she just looked plain. She didn't feel so very grown-up.

The other students were juniors and seniors. They stood in a group around a beautiful, blond girl. She was tall, and her straight, white hair reached her shoulders.

"He put his arm around me, and I said . . ."

Carol stood too far away to hear the end of the story. It disappeared under shouts of laughter.

Carol thought, if I were going to East High, Mary-Lu and I would be pedalling along together. They had biked to East Junior every day for three years. Then Carol remembered Mary-Lu and she were no longer friends. We've had fights before, Carol thought; but this is different, Mary-Lu's changed.

The bus appeared. It stopped right in front of the

beautiful blond. The crowd pushed on and Carol followed last in line. The bus was almost full. All the windows were down, but the noise seemed deafening. Carol paused in confusion. The tall blond blocked the aisle. She leaned from her seat to embrace a friend seated on the other aisle.

"Move along, find a seat," hollered the bus driver over the voices of the students. "You there, little missy, I can't wait all day."

Carol blushed all over. She felt the blood rush in her cheeks, her neck, and even her fingertips.

"Excuse me," she said, but the blond girl ignored her. Carol tried to step over her long legs.

"You'll have to jump," teased a boy seated on the aisle. "Hey, Elisha," he yelled at the blond, "move your designer jeans." Everyone laughed. Carol continued to blush.

. "Oh, I'm so terribly sorry," Elisha purred. She slowly slid her legs out of the way as the bus jolted forward.

The boy caught Carol's arm. "You'd better sit here," he said, moving over and pulling her down beside him.

"Thanks," she replied breathlessly.

"Don't mind Elisha. She just thinks she's the star of West Egelton High School," he dropped his voice to a whisper, "but she's due for one big surprise." He laughed to himself.

Carol's confusion deepened. "She is?"

"Oh," he grinned, "let me introduce myself. No good playing white knight if the lady doesn't know your name. I'm Leonard Whitkins."

"Witless to his friends," cracked Elisha from across the aisle.

"Some people dig their graves with their mouths," he smiled. "Len to my friends," he said to Carol.

"My name's Carol Clark. I'm a sophomore."

"Just move to Egelton?"

"No, I went to East Junior, but they changed the district lines."

"Lucky for us," he said. He seemed to be studying her.

Carol felt her blush returning. She decided to ignore it. She studied him in return. He had light brown hair that hung uncut over his dark brown eyes. His skin was pale. He wore a plaid shirt from which the two top buttons were missing. But it was ironed and neatly tucked into his jeans.

"You could be just perfect," he said at last.

"What?" she asked, not sure she had heard him correctly. How could someone so messy accuse her of anything?

"I meant for my play," Len explained.

"Your play?" Carol asked.

"I don't seem to be able to begin at the beginning of anything," he laughed again. "Maybe I should start over," he shook Carol's hand. "Hello, my name's Len. I wrote the winter play for the Drama Club. It has a part for you. Won't you please, please, please, please, please, try out?"

Carol suspected that if they weren't on a moving bus, he might have knelt on one knee.

"I had planned to try out," she replied.

"Good, great," he smiled. "Do you have any experience?" he asked as the bus stopped in front of the school.

"Oh, yes, I played the rabbit in *Alice in Wonderland* and Sutter's daughter in *The Gold Rush Story*."

"That's wonderful!" he exclaimed as he pushed her into the line of exiting students.

She noticed that he was only a little taller than herself, not more than five-foot-five, she judged.

11

Len did not say goodbye. He left the bus humming under his breath and hurried toward a side entrance.

He's nice, but sort of strange, Carol concluded. She wondered about the ironed shirt with its missing buttons. What would he have done if I said no to the audition?

"May I have your card, please?" asked a student hall guard at the front entrance.

Carol searched her shoulder bag. She handed him the postcard with her homeroom assignment.

"Follow the hallway to the right of the courtyard, past the auditorium. Room 101 is in the other side of the small gym."

Carol admired her new school. The brick covered lobby had one glass wall overlooking a sculpture garden. That must be the courtyard, she thought. A large sign on the glass doors said "Honor Students Only!" She turned right around the corner of the auditorium and walked past the small gym to Room 101. It said "Health Education" on the wooden door. As she entered, a loud buzzer sounded.

"Five minute warning," said the teacher over the low murmur of the new students. "At the main bell, I shall begin to seat you."

Carol settled at a desk near the front of the room. She thought, here I go again; this is going to be awful. Getting seated was always the worst part of school. Over the past three years Carol had learned to hate the first day of the term. When the students stood in size-order for desks, she was always first in line. By the end of the day the other kids would tease her. She knew it was coming. She pretended not to care.

The buzzer sounded again. The teacher said, "Anderson, first desk by the door."

Carol could hardly believe her ears. Even in alphabetical order she would be in the front row, but she did not have to stand at the front of a size-order line. The first day horror was gone. When her name was called, she smiled and took the seat by the window.

Mr. Brockton, the teacher, was a heavy, gray-haired man. He wore a brown suit with a white shirt and a maroon tie. When the class was seated, he explained, "This period will be extended today. You will receive your class cards and some other materials about West Egelton High School."

His formal manner impressed the class. They listened and obeyed. They filled out green, yellow, and pink cards with their programs. They signed the computer punch cards and took the health forms for their parents to sign.

Carol's hand began to ache. She shook it.

"Miss Clark, do you have a question?"

"No, sir," Carol responded, surprised, "I mean, yes, what subject do you teach?"

"Trigonometry and honors mathematics," he replied. "I imagine I shall see some of you in my classes next term."

They took turns reading aloud from the school hand-book. Just before the bell rang, he gave them their locker keys.

"You will find your lockers opposite this classroom. The keys are in numerical order. If there is any problem, I will deal with it tomorrow morning. You may go when the buzzer sounds. I will expect you back here at noon."

Carol was glad to find her locker key worked. She did not want to discuss any problems with Mr. Brockton.

Classes were reduced to twenty minutes each. That was barely enough time to be seated and hand in computer cards. Each teacher listed books and materials the students were expected to buy and bring to class. By noon Carol had attended five shortened classes, and her head was spinning. The loudspeaker announced it was time to return to homeroom. A half hour assembly to welcome the new sophomore class was scheduled to end the first day at West Egelton Senior High School.

As she walked toward her homeroom past the auditorium, Carol saw David White. He looks like a sun god, she thought, observing his bronze curls and deep tan. Suddenly he broke into a big smile and started to wave. A thrill ran through Carol; her skin felt cold and hot at the same time. The tall, handsome senior seemed really glad to see her. She rushed along the hall.

"Hi, David," she said smiling with pleasure, just as he called, "Elisha, you look good enough to eat."

"Anytime you want," murmured the stunning blond. She stepped from behind Carol. In her haste Elisha knocked the notebook from Carol's hands.

"It must have been a long, lonely summer," replied the doctor's son, bending to pick up the notebook. As he handed it back to Carol he paused. "You're Carol Clark, aren't you?"

"Yes," she answered, pleased that he remembered her at last.

"Your mother phoned mine last night. She asked me to watch out for you."

"She did?" Carol said it in dismay before she could stop herself. She squeezed her notebook wishing she could hide under it.

"Yes," he smiled. "If you have any questions, I'll be glad to help. The first few days can be awful confusing."

"David, honey, we'll be late," insisted Elisha, slipping her arm around his and drawing him through the stage entrance. As the door closed, Carol overheard, "On the bus, that little . . ."

Little, Carol thought, next to her anyone's little; but the image of David and Elisha arm in arm distressed her.

"You didn't say you knew David White." Len ap-

14

peared out of the crowd. Carol was startled.

"Oh, he's my doctor's son."

"Yeah? Around here he's our leading man."

"Will he be in your play?"

"Our play," he laughed. "Sure, he's in everything. I've got to hurry. The Drama Club officers run these assemblies," he turned, "I'll see you tomorrow on the bus; I have to stay late today."

Carol hurried along the hall to room 101. She compared the boys. Len's strangeness made her feel comfortable. David's graciousness made her feel uncomfortable. The bell rang just as she reached her desk. Safe, she thought, looking up. Mr. Brockton began taking the roll. Several students arrived after the buzzer.

When he finished calling the names, he said, "You are late if you are not in your seat when I call your name; if you are late three times, I send your name to the detention committee. And you may argue your case with them."

The class lined up in pairs. At the bell they moved silently out the door along the hall and into the auditorium.

Carol realized that in high school everyone is treated as a child regardless of size.

Her class sat near the front in the center section of the orchestra. Carol approved of the lemon yellow walls and the lawn green curtains. The school colors, she remembered, after noticing several football flags decorating the stage.

The lights dimmed; the curtains opened. A giant American flag hung in the center of the stage. And directly in front of it stood David White.

Carol felt her cheeks burn. How could Mother have told him to watch me; he's so good looking. I don't want to have him think I'm a baby. . . .

"Welcome, sophomores of West Egelton High School," David began. "My name is David White, and as president of the Drama Club, which plans these assemblies, I am privileged to be the first to formally greet you as fellow students." He paused. "Now, please rise, and Elisha Hudson, the Drama Club vice-president, will lead the pledge of allegiance." He walked to the right.

Elisha stood to the left of the flag. She wore a bright green robe over her jeans and sweater. Carol got to her feet with the rest of the students, but the perfect balance of the sun god, David, and the snow queen, Elisha, made Carol forget the words of the pledge.

The flag was raised, and behind it the school orchestra and glee club performed the national anthem. They, too, wore green robes over their clothing.

When the students settled into their seats, the stage filled with flip-flopping cheerleaders. The audience shouted and clapped with energetic enjoyment. Carol had difficulty paying attention, until David reappeared. He introduced the president of the student union, who introduced the principal. While he spoke, Carol's attention slipped away.

She tried to imagine herself in a dark, green robe at David's side; the jolly green midget, she thought. Carol could not even imagine herself on that huge stage. The auditorium was much larger than the junior high school utility room, where she had performed in the past. How could Len think she would be chosen to act in his play?

Carol felt a hand on her shoulder; she looked up, startled. The girl next to her was standing. She pointed toward the aisle.

"Miss Clark," said Mr. Brockton, "school's over, you can go home to sleep."

Carol realized the program had ended. She jumped to

her feet wondering if she had missed anything important. She tried to remember—had Len been on the stage? Had she seen him? The only image Carol could recall was that of David's golden good looks.

chapter
⋆⋆⋆ 3 ⋆⋆⋆

"Higher, Carol, higher everyone," yelled Elisha. "Now, one more time; and one and two and one and two."

The rows of dance students kicked their way across the small gym. Sweat flew off their moving bodies. Carol felt as wrung out and smelly as an old sponge. Her dark curls hung limply against her face and neck. They dripped salt water into her eyes.

"Who put her in charge?" whispered a senior in the row behind Carol's.

"No one puts Elisha in charge, she was born that way," responded the small redheaded junior next to Carol.

"There will be a revolt if she keeps this class over-time."

Carol listened to the hiss of complaints around her. She had not noticed that the others found the class difficult. Even if Elisha had not arranged the class in size order with Carol first in the front row, her struggle to keep up would have prevented her from noticing.

"Dance was supposed to be easier than hockey!"

"This is the hardest class she's given," observed the redhead.

"She's sure got some bee in her bustle today."

The giggles brought on a general gasping for air among those who heard the comment.

"You in the front, no talking," ordered Elisha, eyeing Carol's end of the line. "We'll try it again with the music."

"What does she mean 'we'; she isn't moving!" stated the senior.

"No sweat on Elisha," cracked someone Carol could not see.

Carol had been surprised and disappointed by the calisthenic nature of her dance class.

"Every Tuesday and Thursady I fall asleep on the bus."

"I just about make it home, myself," the redhead responded.

"Good thing this is the last class of the day."

"Save your breath for dancing! You won't feel so tired," Elisha snapped at Carol's row as they moved past her.

The bell rang. Students bolted for the locker rooms. The whistle blew. "Finish your cross, then line up against the wall."

"To be shot?" shouted the senior.

"She wouldn't put us out of our misery," whispered the junior.

"Until Miss Jenkins dismisses the class." Elisha tapped on the office window. The class watched Miss Jenkins place her coffee cup on the desk and walk to the door.

"An excellent class, Elisha; girls, please give a round of applause to show your appreciation." The response was somewhat limp.

"This is the last week of modern dance; you have one more class. Next Tuesday Tanya Greene will take over . . ." A loud burst of applause interrupted her. "That's very nice, girls. Tanya will be teaching four weeks of Jazz Dance. Anyone who wants to continue with modern dance may join the Modern Dance Club. It meets here every Monday afternoon."

The class edged toward the exits.

"And don't forget the pep rally, Friday right after school! I expect you all to be there! Class dismissed."

"Ten minutes after the bell. I don't believe it!"

"I'll miss the bus," shouted a girl pulling jeans and a jacket over her sweaty leotards and tights.

"Did you see Elisha slip out?" asked a girl, stripping as she spoke.

"She has to run the Drama Club auditions," answered the redhead.

"Yeah, but I'll be glad when she sweats along with the rest of us," replied her now towel-wrapped friend.

Carol looked unhappily at her reflection. A shower could not make her feel any wetter. It might make her feel better, but it would not improve her hair. She had made a special effort to look good for the auditions, but Elisha's class had undone her work completely.

"Aren't you showering?" asked the girl in the towel.

"No," replied the junior, "I don't want to be late for the auditions."

Carol recalled that Len had warned her not to be late. "If you're late you'll miss the description of the plot and characters."

Both she and Elisha had asked for advance information. He took advantage of their curiosity to tease them. But after almost four weeks on the bus, Carol knew nothing more than Len had told her on the first day. And that was more than he had told Elisha.

Voices drifted over the banks of brown metal lockers.

"Would you rather take hockey?"

"Doesn't Miss Jenkins ever teach?"

"Sure, the last four weeks—tumbling."

"That's not dance!"

"It's called gymnastic ballet."

Carol slipped into a shower stall. The running water cut off conversation. I'll only be a little later than I already am, she thought. I can't go to the audition covered in sweat. By four-thirty I'd be so stinky, they wouldn't let me on the late bus.

Dressed in her jeans and black turtleneck, Carol rubbed her hair with the damp towel. Almost everyone had left the locker room. The hot water brought bright color into her cheeks. The dampness darkened her hair, brows, and lashes.

"You're late, I was afraid you chickened out," Len whispered when she entered the near empty auditorium.

"I'm sorry, Elisha worked the dance class double hard."

"I'll bet!" he smiled. "You look beautiful—like an antique china doll."

"Thank you!"

"I just wish you'd worn something more, more..." he searched for the word, "more female."

"Funny, you don't look like my mother," Carol replied. "Did I miss the descriptions?"

"Yes, they're just getting ready to start the readings," Len replied. "You better sign the list."

As Carol moved down the aisle he added, "You sign for Mandy."

Elisha stood at the front of the auditorium. Next to her on the lip of the stage lay eight clipboards.

"Mandy?" asked Carol. Her still damp hair made her feel self-conscious as she stood under the gaze of Elisha.

"Yes, of course," replied the other girl, pointing to the third clipboard.

Carol signed. She noticed that there was only one

other signature on Mandy's board, while the other characters' boards held as many as a dozen names. It must be a small part Carol decided.

"Pages fifteen and thirty-four," said Elisha.

"What?" responded Carol.

"Over there," Elisha pointed at something behind Carol's back with impatience.

Carol turned around. The top of the grand piano was covered with piles of paper. Pages from the script, she realized.

"Excuse me, Elisha, what were those numbers again, please?"

"They're on the clipboard," snapped Elisha.

Carol leaned over the boards. "Fifteen and thirty-four, thank you."

Carol took the pages and sat in the front row. A few seats to her right she saw a junior boy from her French class. He was holding hands with the talkative redhead from her dance class. Carol noticed that the redhead still wore her sky blue tights and leotard under a ruffled purple skirt. She had added a scarf and some bangles to create the frilly, little girl look Carol now tried to avoid.

Shifting in her seat, Carol was surprised at how many of the auditioning students she knew. Almost half of her drama class sat scattered around the auditorium. Three girls from Carol's English class giggled and waved when she caught their eyes. A boy she met through Len turned thumbs up at her from the center of the auditorium. Behind him sat Mr. Carter, her drama teacher and the Drama Club sponsor. He regularly encouraged students to participate in the club.

On Mr. Carter's left sat a dark-haired senior girl. Carol had seen her bringing messages to Mr. Carter during class. On Mr. Carter's right sat David White. Even in the dimness of the half-lit auditorium, his golden waves

22

glowed. Carol felt her pulse rate increase. The blood rushed to her cheeks as it did every time she saw him. The memory of her mother's phone call upset Carol each time they met. She usually avoided him and prayed that David would forget about her and her mother's instructions.

"Has everyone signed? Last chance!" Mr. Carter waited a moment. No one responded. "All right, Elisha, please bring me the lists."

Elisha released the lists from the clipboards and carried them to Mr. Carter. The rattle of script sheets sounded like static from a high voltage wire.

Carol skimmed her two pages. One represented a first meeting between her character, Mandy, and a boy named Chris in a classroom. Mandy had been assigned to coach Chris in English. Carol was impressed. The conversation sounded easy and natural, at least on paper. She realized that she had never stopped to consider if Len was a good writer or not.

She read the second sheet and concluded that Len was a very good writer. The second sheet described a fight between Mandy and her English teacher about the tutoring assignment. Carol shifted the pages nervously. In junior high the parts had been chosen by the teacher. She had never had to audition before.

Nancy, Mr. Carter's dark-haired assistant, called the names of two boys. They climbed the steps at the front of the auditorium. A folding table and two metal chairs stood in front of a black velvet curtain.

"Begin when you feel ready," said Mr. Carter. "I'll tell you when to switch parts."

Carol did not know what he meant; the boys seemed to understand. They read about ten lines each, then Mr. Carter stopped them. They repeated the scene, each boy reading the role he had not read.

How could Mr. Carter decide anything in so little time? Carol wondered. She was glad she would be reading with boys. Mr. Carter could not expect her to switch roles. She reread her scenes. It's a good thing Mandy's a small part, she thought. I'd hate to read against Elisha. Carol considered the difference in their sizes. She smiled glumly as the idea of her small part took on a double meaning.

Five pairs of boys read the same scene ten times. Some seemed more awkward than others, but Carol knew she could not really distinguish between them.

"All right, let's have some variety," Mr. Carter announced.

The dark, senior girl called two of the girls from Carol's English class.

They read a giggling scene full of gossip and whispers. The third girl read with a senior from Carol's drama class. Altogether Carol counted fourteen girls. She noticed they had not exchanged roles, which made the reading move faster.

"Now, let's see the Mr. Dickersons," Mr. Carter suggested. His assistant called the names of three pairs of boys; one tall, and one short boy read in each pair. The scene was an argument between the teacher and the boy, Chris. In the last pair David White played the teacher.

Carol stopped rereading her scenes to study the handsome senior.

Mr. Carter asked, "David, please stay on stage, I want to see the Janes and Mandys each read against the same Mr. Dickerson."

At the mention of Mandy, Carol became nervous. She sat up in her chair and grasped the white sheets of paper. But Mr. Carter chose to see the Janes first.

Carol watched each girl as she stood beside David

White. No, she concluded, Mr. Carter would never choose me to act with David.

"Elisha, would you please read for the part of Jane," requested Mr. Carter.

"I don't feel well," replied the stunning junior.

"Do your best," Mr. Carter insisted.

Carol watched as Elisha strolled slowly up onto the stage. The two tall blonds read side by side just as they had done during last month's assembly. No, Carol repeated to herself, Mr. Carter would never choose me. David and Elisha are the perfect couple.

The perfect couple hissed at each other in whispers. But sitting in the front row, Carol could not hear their words. The obvious anger between them reached every person in the auditorium.

Mr. Carter interrupted the fight, "Thank you, Elisha, you can come down now. We'll go on to Mandy."

Carol prepared to spring out of her seat. But the red-haired junior from the dance class was called first. She had read earlier for the role of one of the giggling gossips.

Carol listened to the way the junior read the argument with David; the real fight a few moments before made the reading seem hollow. Carol realized that the emotion, not the words, carried the meaning to the audience.

"Carol Clark," called Mr. Carter's assistant. Carol jumped to her feet and hurried toward the stairs. The stage looked huge from the auditorium seats; but now Carol felt like she was in a small room. She could hardly catch her breath in the tiny space in which she stood.

David smiled, "Hi, Carol, I haven't seen you around much. How are you doing?"

Carol's pulse was already racing. She smiled, afraid to speak. Her first word would squeak; everyone would laugh. She knew it.

David continued, "I'm sorry. I told your Mom I'd watch out for you; I haven't had much time."

Suddenly Carol felt her temper rise. Why does Mother have to make a fool out of me all the time?

"Whenever you're ready," said Mr. Carter.

David read the first line. Carol responded. The anger flowed into her voice; she did not hear it. By the time she finished the page Carol felt both better and worse. The anger was gone. But her knees were shaking.

"That was great," David said.

Carol was already walking off the stage. The next thing she knew, Carol found herself in the lobby. Her English classmates were giggling and hugging her.

"That was wonderful!"

"How did you have the courage?"

"I could never have read for the lead."

"Isn't David White wonderful?"

"The lead?" Carol asked. "I thought Mandy was a small part."

"Didn't you hear the description?"

"You mean you didn't know!"

"You were wonderful," said Len, taking Carol's hand. "I knew you were the right girl for Mandy as soon as I saw you on the bus."

"The bus!" screeched Carol's three classmates. "Come on, we'll be late."

Carol, Len, and the three girls started for the doors.

"Carol, Carol wait, please," David White shouted to her from the auditorium door.

"Eee!" squealed the other girls, "Go on, we'll hold your bus."

"I can't, I'll miss the bus," Carol called over her shoulder as she ran.

"Oh, Carol, how could you?"

"Stop acting like he's a rock star," Carol gasped at her companions as they ran.

"David White's better than a rock star!"

"He's dreamy."

"They're silly," said Len as Carol and he boarded their bus, "but David sure loves it."

chapter
. 4 *.*

As the bus bounced and jolted Carol flipped through the pages of her notebook. Although she had a history quiz, it was not the Bill of Rights that concerned her. She stared at her neat handwriting on the blue lined pages; however, she saw nothing, her mind was preoccupied with the West Egelton High School Drama Club.

"Hey, Carol, looks like Elisha's run off with your boyfriend," teased the girl seated behind her.

Carol turned from her books to look at Laura, a sophomore she knew from French One. "Boyfriend? I don't have a boyfriend!" Her mind leaped to the image of David and Elisha side by side in the hall, during the assembly, and at the audition.

"She means Len," said Susan, sitting in the seat beside Laura. She leaned forward shifting the violin case that she carried everywhere. "Those two have been missing for a couple of days."

"No wonder the bus has been so quiet!" shouted Carla-Ann, the girl seated next to Carol, into the usual morning din.

"They're casting Len's play," Carol cut into their giggles.

"Maris from our English class says you gave a really great audition," commented Carla-Ann.

"Do you think you'll get a part?" yelled Susan, the wavering in her voice reflecting the sudden movement of the bus across an unexpected series of potholes.

"I don't know; the list goes up this morning."

"We'll keep our fingers crossed for you," Laura held up two fists of double-knotted fingers.

The other two girls quickly followed Laura's example.

"Thanks!" Carol shouted over the usual bus noise and the fits of laughter as her three friends tried to link arms. Carol turned away from their silliness. She reopened her loose-leaf and tried to concentrate on her notes.

"Cramming for Edward's history quiz?" asked Patsy when her laughter subsided.

"Emmm himm," affirmed Carol without looking away from her book.

"That must be how you get all those good marks!"

Carla-Ann rearranged herself to face Laura and Patsy. Carol ignored the rest of their conversation.

No, I didn't get a part, she thought unhappily. Mr. Carter didn't even call me back in front of the club for final tryouts. I wish no one knew I wanted to be in the show. Why did Len and everyone have to make such a big deal out of it? They could never pick me to play opposite David.

The image of the tall, golden-haired senior was the focus of Carol's disappointment. She imagined David as she had seen him last, chasing after her when she left the auditorium, his curls disarranged, and his bronzed skin flushed from exertion.

It was a moment Carol had relived many times in the last two days. Each time she experimented with a different ending. Sometimes, David told her, her audition was brilliant and she had won the lead; sometimes he declared his undying devotion and swept her into his arms.

Why choose a dark runt when they could have platinum, model perfect Elisha! She always does everything

29

with such flare. Even her clothing is dramatic! Carol mentally compared her own apple red cardigan with Elisha's fire-engine red cape; her boy's department, army-navy denims with Elisha's skintight designer jeans; and her dark, cotton turtlenecks with Elisha's pastel angora sweaters.

The bus lurched to a stop. Carol closed her notebook and followed the other sophomore girls into the school's main entrance.

"Hey, good luck."

"We'll say we knew you when."

Carol barely heard their good wishes. She was wondering, again, if her mother could be right? A frilly, fluffy, little girl in ruffles might stand out better against all that flair and elegance. But Carol knew the cost of looking like a cute, little girl would be to be treated like one. Anyway, no one who found Elisha attractive, she thought of David again, would even look twice at a pipsqueak like me!

Rounding the corner of the auditorium, Carol saw a bunch of students clustered in front of the Drama Club bulletin board. She recognized Marris and Peggy from her English class, as well as Len's friend, Mark, and Val, the redhead from her dance class.

I may have to pass it; but I don't have to look at it, she thought, skirting the crowd.

"Our leading lady," announced Mr. Carter, emerging from the press of students. They surged forward to read the list he had just posted.

"Carol, come back, where are you going?" Mr. Carter paused with his back to the group of young people.

At the mention of her name Carol spun around to face her teacher. The crowd continued to study the list. Carol heard their cries and exclamations. No one seemed aware of her presence, or her conversation with Mr. Carter.

30

"I have to be seated at the bell, or my homeroom teacher, Mr. Brockton, marks me late!" she explained. Carol wished the warning bell would sound, so she could dash away from this scene of her obvious failure.

"Don't worry about that; just ask my assistant, Nancy, for a pass," said Mr. Carter, placing a package of tacks in the pocket of his tweed wool jacket.

"A pass?" Carol wondered why Mr. Carter thought she would need a pass. They were usually given to students called to the main office for messages or disciplinary matters. Then Carol remembered, Drama Club members were expected to run errands for the department. "Was there something you wanted me to do?"

"Certainly, go pick up your script. We start rehearsal on Monday, right after school."

"My script?" She wondered if the club had assigned her a crew position.

"Hey, Carol, congratulations, the best girl won!" exclaimed redheaded Val as she slipped out of the mass of acting hopefuls. "I'll be seeing you at rehearsals!" She walked quickly toward the lobby.

"Did I get a part?" Carol asked Mr. Carter in confusion.

"Didn't David tell you?"

"I haven't seen him since the audition. When I didn't get a callback I didn't think you..."

"You're Mandy. I sent David after you to say that you wouldn't need a second reading."

"He followed me, but...Mandy! That's the lead, isn't it?" her voice rose to an excited squeak.

"Yes, and Nancy has your script in the office."

"I'll go right over."

"Good, I'll see you in class." Mr. Carter walked toward the stage door. Just before it closed, he poked his head out, "Oh, yes, congratulations, Carol!"

31

She edged back around the group at the bulletin board. Then she stopped and turned. Carol slipped in among the students and worked her way forward to the wall. It was true. Just as Mr. Carter had said. There was her name at the top of the list.

"Congratulations, Carol," said a boy whose name she had forgotten.

"Yeah, it was a great audition," commented a girl Carol could not see.

Carol studied the list along with the others. Suddenly, her breath caught in her throat. Just below her name was typed, David White—Mr. Dickerson. Seeing their names so close together sent a tingling sensation down her back. Carol realized the club had picked her to play opposite David, and she would be seeing him every day at rehearsal.

Glancing over the rest of the list, Carol noted who among her friends she should be congratulating. Maris, Peggy, and Lenore, the three girls from her English class, as well as Val, the redhead who had tried out for Mandy, would be playing the small roles of gossiping students. Elisha had been assigned the part of Jane Thomas. And Frank, Len's friend, would be Chris, the boy Mandy was supposed to tutor.

None of the other names were familiar. Carol smiled; I'll know them soon enough. She wiggled out of the crowd, crushing at least one set of toes in her efforts to free herself.

"Maris, I'm glad you're going to be in the show," Carol greeted her friend.

"Thanks, we all knew you would be," answered the raven-haired sophomore, shifting her surprisingly large pile of books.

"I didn't. In fact, when I wasn't called back, I thought I hadn't made it at all."

"Well, you did, and I think you really deserve it."

"Thank you." Carol was delighted and amazed at her friend's loyal support. "Where's Peggy? I thought I saw her just a minute ago."

"You probably did, but she had to go. Her homeroom's near the cafeteria."

"I'll see her in English."

"I'll see you there, too." Maris hurried down the corridor.

Carol crossed the hall and entered the drama department office. Mr. Carter's dark-haired assistant sat behind a gray, metal desk on which stood two phones and multiple stacks of papers. She wore a brilliantly colored, hand-embroidered peasant blouse; her hair hung in heavy braids.

"Hi, Carol, congratulations!"

"Thank you; are you Nancy?" inquired Carol, admiring the quiet sense of authority the older girl projected.

"Yes, Nancy Rodgers, Mr. C's senior aide."

"He told me you'd give me a pass and a script."

Nancy lifted some of the pages from a nearby pile. "This is the first act of *Extracurricular*. If you can wait a few minutes, the second act will be delivered from the printing office."

"Do you have a stapler?" asked Carol, accepting the loose pages.

"Yes, but you'd better use a clip-on plastic binder or a small loose-leaf. That way you can separate the pages you're not using and insert rehearsal notes.

"I hadn't thought of . . ." Carol stopped talking when Nancy lifted the buzzing intercom.

"Drama department, Nancy Rodgers speaking." She signalled for Carol to sit on a brown, metal folding chair.

"Fine, send them down . . . I have students waiting for them." Nancy smiled at Carol. "Oh, all right!" She rolled her eyes toward the ceiling. "I'll have to get someone to cover the desk, but I'll be there as soon as I can." She dropped the receiver like a bad test grade.

"Carol, I have to pick up the second act from the print shop. Would you mind watching the desk for a few minutes?"

The warning bell rang. Carol responded with a self-conscious jolt. "I don't think I should; I really don't want to be late."

"No problem! The passes are in Mr. C's office. And I'll be here before homeroom ends." Nancy crossed the office. Her dark corduroy skirt rippled around the top of her elaborately tooled boots.

"I really don't think this is a good idea," Carol whispered nervously, as she perched uncomfortably at the edge of the desk chair.

Nancy reassured her, "Just answer the phones and say I'll be right back." She opened the door. "I will, you know!" and she smiled at Carol's seriousness.

From the time the door shut behind Nancy, Carol stared grimly at the phones. She willed them not to ring. At any moment she expected the solid figure of Mr. Brockton to burst into the room with exclamations of how he had found her out. When the homeroom bell sounded, her hand grabbed the receiver in a reflex movement. Recognizing her own foolishness, Carol laughed and told herself to relax.

She reached for the first act of Len's play, *Extracurricular*. She read the title page and paused to consider what a special friend Len had become for her. He's sincere and funny. And kind, too, she thought. I'm really glad I was chosen to be in his play. It seemed so important to him. She turned to the character descriptions and added, he's really a good person.

Mr. Dickerson—He is a tall, attractive, intelligent man of 35. He teaches English at Midwood High, where he has taught for eleven years. He enjoys his work. He dates the school secretary, Jane Thomas. His clothing tends to be sporting: corduroy pants, turtlenecks, sweaters, or jackets with leather elbow patches.

Mandy Richards—She is small, cute, and bubbly. She is a freshman, but seems younger because of her sweet innocence. She wears bright colors and ruffles.

Carol stopped reading in disbelief. She reread Len's description of Mandy. She read it three times while the lump in her chest brought tears to her eyes. Anger and disappointment fought with her self-control.

How could Len do this to me? The character of Mandy is everything I don't want to be. I can't go in front of the whole school as cute and bubbly! I won't! I'd die first! It's not fair. Carol protested silently while rereading the dreadful sentences. Each time she hoped the cruel, disappointing description would change.

The lead in a play should be beautiful and clever, not cute and innocent! David is tall, attractive and intelligent...David, oh, no, David...he must really think I'm cute and innocent. No wonder he took Mom's request to look after me seriously! Why did this have to happen to me? It's not fair! If only I'd grow...if only, I weren't so small. Five feet is not a normal height for a woman! Carol answered her mother's too often repeated assertion.

"Well, Little Miss Muffet, I see you're taking over the office, too." Elisha leaned against the desk. Her midnight blue jump suit set off her silver hair. She tapped her magenta nails in a drum roll on the dark green desk blotter.

Carol blinked back her tears and swallowed hard. The lump threatened to choke her. She wondered if Elisha heard her gulp.

"Hello, Elisha, congratulations; Nancy's picking up the scripts. She'll be right back."

The stunning blond ran the points of her nails across the soft cardboard. The pressure left grooves, and the sound raised the hairs on Carol's neck. "She can take her time! There won't be many congratulations when Len's turkey opens."

"What's wrong with Len's play?" In spite of her own, personal doubts, Carol defended her friend's work. "The parts I read are extremely well written."

"Not for this school," Elisha looked down at Carol. "Of course, you wouldn't know; you didn't hear the debates over the character of Mandy."

Carol felt herself begin to fidget under the stare of Elisha's icy blue eyes. She forced the unintentional movements to look casual and tucked the first act papers into the back of her loose-leaf notebook.

"The officers of the Drama Club had a meeting; we all agreed, there was no one in West Egelton Senior who could play the part of Mandy. And, of course, there's no way to cast it, realistically; I mean for the student-teacher relationship to work." She made a rippling gesture of her fingers. So there was no point in asking Len to rewrite it.

"He very graciously offered to withdraw the script." Elisha stretched her body across the desk until she loomed over Carol. "Then David made one of his brilliant suggestions. Why not use someone who just looks the part?"

Carol gathered her books. Her hands shook and her vision blurred.

"Well, we were all ready to search the junior high when you showed up. It was so clever of Len to recruit you. And you certainly are a precious, little thing. I know you'll look just adorable on stage."

Carol walked to the door determined not to give Elisha the satisfaction of seeing her cry. "As long as you're sitting on the desk, you can cover the phones." Carol was astonished to see Elisha's face respond to her accidental witticism. "And please tell Nancy I had to leave."

The empty hall echoed with the sound of Carol's footsteps as she ran toward her homeroom. She hung on the doorknob to catch her breath. Her thoughts continued to race.

I don't look fluffy or frilly! I haven't worn any little girl clothes to school. Maybe Len really did talk to me just to cast his play. It was almost the first thing he told me. I suppose being short, is being short. But, it's so unfair. I'm not sweet and innocent!

"Sleeping Beauty, I presume," pronounced Mr. Brockton, as she stepped into the room.

The class laughed. Carol found herself staring at them in blank confusion like an actress who had forgotten her lines.

"Miss Clark, you're late!" thundered her homeroom teacher. She jumped to face him. The class laughed again.

Carol clutched her books and tried to breathe. "I'm sorry, I had to stop at the drama office."

"May I see your pass?"

"I forgot to get one," Carol whispered in dismay.

"First demerit."

"Oh, Mr. Brockton, I'm sorry! I'll bring it later; I'll . . ."

"No good being sorry, just take your seat."

37

Carol stumbled across the front of the room. She felt thirty-five pairs of eyes watch her clumsy movements. She sunk into her seat just in time to hide the first trickling tear.

The bell rang. The other students rushed for the door. The room emptied. Carol lifted her books and walked slowly behind the crowd.

She watched the hall clear, but couldn't force herself to go to class. Slowly, slowly, she moved at half speed past the tall, green lockers, past the stage door, past the Drama Club bulletin board.

The recently posted cast list caught the breeze and waved as if it were trying to attract Carol's attention. She paused to re-examine her ironic victory.

I won because I looked the part; I won because I happened to take Len's bus. I won because David suggested using a cute junior-high student. Every time we rehearse, he's going to look at me and think . . .

"Carol, I knew you could do it!" Len's voice switched from jubilation to concern, "What's the matter, you look awful!"

"Oh, Len, I didn't even see you." Carol straightened her back and blinked to clear her eyes.

"You don't seem to be seeing much of anything. What's the matter?" He put his hand on her arm and guided her toward the drama office. "Come, sit down. It's my free period; we can talk."

Recognizing the place, Carol pulled back. "No, I have to go to class."

"You're much too upset! Come in for a minute and Mr. C. will give you a pass."

A loud, uncontrolled peel of laughter broke into their quiet conversation. Carol turned to see who the third person was. After a frightened glance up and down the corridor she realized the laughter had been her own.

Both crying and laughing at the same time she said, "Oh, no, not another pass! I didn't get the first one. I forgot. Mr. Brockton gave me a demerit. He wouldn't believe me. I tried to tell him . . ."

"Wait, slow down, take a deep breath," Len held both of her hands and squeezed them hard.

She stopped talking to follow his directions.

"That's good; now take another one, and another. Good."

Carol smiled weakly up at Len. She liked the strength of his hands pressing gently on hers. "I'm sorry, that's never happened before."

"Do you want to talk about it?"

"I'm not sure." Carol noticed again that Len was only a little taller than she but he managed to look as old as any other upperclass student. Done with mirrors, no doubt, she thought and smiled.

"You seem a little better now." He opened the office door. "Would you like to come in?"

"I don't know; but it's late, and I guess I need that pass. I'd hate to get two demerits on the same day."

As she followed him into the office Carol was again presented with the mystery of Len's wardrobe. The right hem of his carefully pressed pants dragged a tail of loose threads and binding ribbon.

"Len, the second act needs . . . oh, our leading lady," David White sat in Nancy's seat behind the gray, metal desk. He stopped checking scripts to greet Carol. "Welcome to the inner sanctum!"

"Hi, David!" Carol wondered if he could see that her eyes were red. She was grateful that Len had helped to calm her down in the hall outside the office.

"I'll get you that pass," Len continued walking across

the room and through the door opposite the hall entrance.

"I've been looking for you for two days. You're one hard lady to catch up with!"

"Really?" Carol felt a surge and a flutter in her chest. She noticed that David's emerald green pullover exactly matched his golden lashed eyes.

"Mr. C. gave me a message for you."

"Yes, he told me, this morning." Her pulse rate dropped.

"Also, I wondered if you might like to see a movie on Saturday night? The Festival's playing *Citizen Kane*."

"With you?"

"Would you prefer going with somebody else?" He asked with what Carol found astonishing self-assurance.

"I mean, is it a date?"

"I asked first."

"Yes, of course, I'd absolutely love to..." Carol broke into giggles of embarrassment over her own enthusiasm.

David, also, laughed. "Nice to meet a girl who knows what she wants," he teased.

Len opened the inner door. "I was about to apologize for taking so long, but I seem to be missing all the fun."

Carol started to explain, "David said..."

But before she could complete her sentence, David cut her off. "I'm afraid it was just one of those things you have to experience." He winked at Carol. "Retelling would spoil it for all of us."

"I wouldn't want anyone to say I spoiled my stars," Len replied lightly. "But, unfortunately, the reason I've lost out on this experience is the pass book seems to have vanished."

"Did you look on the shelf behind the desk?" asked David.

"And under the phone, and in the drawer..."

"That's okay," Carol smiled, "If I hurry, I might not get marked down."

"The bell rang fifteen minutes ago," protested Len.

"I can tell Mr. C. to send you a pass later," offered David.

"That would be great. Thank you, David." Carol fought the impulse to fling herself across the desk to reward him with a kiss. She hardly noticed Len's comment.

"Some teachers won't accept a late pass."

Carol opened the door into the hall. Her book pile felt lighter, the air smelled sweeter, and everything seemed possible. She was surprised when Len followed her out into the corridor.

"Carol, are you all right now?" he asked with concern.

She started walking briskly away, "Sure, I'm just fine. I never felt better!" she called back over her shoulder without looking at Len.

She arrived at her history class twenty-five minutes late. The quiz was over. Carol barely heard Dr. Edward's reprimand; the second demerit hardly registered.

chapter
✦✦ 5 ✦✦

Rainbows shimmered on Carol's face. The light woke her. She stretched and readjusted the pink, thermal blanket to shade her eyes. Suddenly she sat up. The rainbows slid along her rose flannel gown.

It's Saturday! she thought, as if this information by itself should be cause for celebration.

Carol reached for the tiny cut crystal ball that hung in her window. She spun it. Pinpoint rainbows swirled across the organdy curtains and the pink and white striped wallpaper in a fantastic almost dizzying dance.

Addressing her soft, woolly, toy unicorn, Carol exclaimed, "I feel like a waltzing rainbow." She leapt from the bed and made a whirling, dipping, bouncing circuit of her bedroom. The lacy ruffles on her nightie flew around her bouncing form. "This is what dance class should be like!" she informed her four-legged, white haired partner and hugged his pliable body tightly in her arms.

Unfortunately, Carol's memory of her elective gym class carried both her disappointment in the nature of the exercises and her frustration at her inability to perform in the way she had imagined that dance class would permit. Her memory also included Elisha, her long, perfect legs demonstrating the impossible steps.

Elisha's image looked up into David's eyes as they strolled arm in arm through the cafeteria. Elisha's image modeled astonishing and dramatic clothing at the bus stop. Elisha's image shattered into an infinity of dust in a ray of morning sunlight as Carol approached her calendar.

There it was, October, illustrated by velvet-bound bouquets of golden mums. The square representing the third Saturday of the month was covered in red magic marker. Carol had drawn stars and hearts to mark her first date, as well as added a neat inscription that read, David White, *Citizen Kane*.

I still don't believe it, but it's true! David asked me to go to the movies! It's almost like a movie. She hugged the shaggy, stuffed animal. I mean, we're both chosen to star in the school play, and then we fall madly in love. Next, of course, a talent scout will discover us and we'll become a famous theatrical couple. . . .

"Carol, are you up?" her mother's voice interrupted the fantasy.

"Yes, I'll be dressed and down in a minute." Carol picked up her alarm clock. Its ten-thirty already? She could hardly believe the curliqued arms pointed to the correct roman numerals.

"That's okay! There's no rush today. Just pick up the phone."

No rush, Carol responded in her mind, as she hurried to the upstairs hall phone. I have to get to the shopping center, choose a dress, find shoes, arrange . . .

"Hello?" said a rich male voice.

"Yes, who is this, please?"

"It's David."

"Oh, David." He's not coming, she cried in her heart. The date's off. I knew it was too good to be true.

"I just wanted to tell you I'll pick you up at your place around seven forty-five."

"Seven forty-five," she repeated breathlessly.

43

"Yeah, that's all right, isn't it? It's not your dinner time or anything."

"It's fine; it's wonderful; it's perfect!"

"You're always so enthusiastic!" They both laughed. "I'll see you later."

"Yes, at seven forty-five."

"Bye."

"Bye, see you later..." She stopped herself from repeating, at seven forty-five, to the silent line.

He called! We're going out! It's really happening! Carol's thoughts danced faster than her feet. She began pulling clothes out of her closet and her drawers.

Should I take a shower now? There's so little time. It's almost eleven; he'll be here at seven forty-five. That's only, let me see, eleven, twelve, thirteen, I mean, one... She counted aloud on her fingers. "Eleven, twelve, one, two, three, four, five, six, seven and forty-five. A little more than eight hours."

If I take a shower now, I'll have to take another later. Of course, if I shower, now, I can wash my hair.... It will be clean and dry when I'm ready to arrange it with Mom's hot rollers. What if she won't let me use them?

While waiting for the water in the upstairs bathroom to run hot, Carol allowed her mind to rush from problem to problem.

"Breakfast's hot! Come and get it!" Mr. Clark's voice interrupted Carol's mental dithering.

"I'll be down as soon as I'm dressed," she called over the upstairs railing.

"The longer you take, the less you'll eat!" Her father's playful warning followed Carol across the hall. She neglected to answer it in her rush to get washed and dressed.

"Well, I see we're having a squeaky, clean girl for breakfast," he observed when Carol approached the dinette set in the kitchen.

"That's funny, they look like pancakes to me!" Carol pushed her damp hair off her face and settled at the table while her family performed their regular weekend dialogue.

"Carol, you didn't dry your hair."

"Mom, it dries just fine by itself."

"Who was the early caller?"

Carol smiled at her father to show her appreciation for his understanding, "David White."

"What time is he picking you up?" asked her mother, removing a heat-proof dish from the oven and placing it on the table in front of Carol.

"Seven forty-five. We're going to see *Citizen Kane*."

"Do my ears deceive me? Is my little girl going on a date?"

"Oh, Daddy, I told you I was going out with David White," she replied, spreading butter and jam on her breakfast.

"You know, dear, Dr. White's son."

"That's all right, then; if there's a disaster, I'm sure he'll take good care of you," pronounced her father, waving his forkful of pancakes for emphasis.

"It's supposed to be a date, not a disaster, but it will be a disaster if I can't get to the mall." Carol attacked her plateful of food. "I have nothing to wear."

"You don't eat like a woman in love," teased Mr. Clark.

"We could try that new discount place," suggested Mrs. Clark. "The Havor girls bought some lovely things there last week."

"If you're trying to fit Carol into their clothes, you'd better give her another helping of pancakes. And heavy on the syrup," he added.

"You two have no kindness of heart. They were very good neighbors. And I'm not sure we did the right thing

45

by staying here; East High has a fine reputation."

"Mom, that's old news," insisted Carol with exasperation. "I love West! It's really wonderful!"

"This is the best breakfast I've had all day!" exclaimed her father.

"You two! You're always in league against your own best interests." Mrs. Clark began to clear the table. "The sooner we clean up the kitchen, the sooner we get to the mall."

Downing a full glass of milk without stopping between swallows, Carol understood her mother's hint and took her place at the sink.

"Many hands make light work," quoted her father as he scraped the plates that her mother had piled on the counter.

"I never understand why I should spend so long to prepare a meal that's over before anyone has time to enjoy it." Mrs. Clark sighed and swept the floor around the feet of her family.

Mr. Clark grabbed his wife and kissed her with a resounding smack. "That's for slaving over a hot stove."

"Oh, Don." Mrs. Clark pushed him away and hurried to the broom closet.

Carol smiled as she placed the last of the glasses in the dishwasher.

"Bus for Greenacher Mall leaving in..." Carol's father looked at her mother.

"Fifteen minutes." She started toward the kitchen door. "Carol, think about what you want! I have to take in the dry cleaning, pick up the groceries, and drop the electric percolator at the Fix-It Shop. There won't be a lot of time for fooling around."

As she wiped the counter Carol thought, that means I'm supposed to pick out the first flowered, frilled, and fussy garment on the rack. And she'll stand over me to make sure I won't waste time trying on anything I might like.

However, when they reached the shopping center, Carol's father dropped her at the new Discount Dress Designs. "Carol, find something you like, and take your time! Your mother and I are going to Queen's Market." He handed her some cash. "We'll pick you up right here in about an hour!"

Her mother's protests followed her up to the giant, sliding, glass doors. Just inside the entrance, Carol stopped and stood still in amazement. The place seemed larger than a supermarket, possibly larger than the school football field. Clothing hung from racks of all sizes and shapes. A long bar of evening gowns was attached to the ceiling. The store looked like a fun-house maze.

But Carol was uncertain about how much fun it would be. Women with parcels and strollers blocked every aisle. Small children darted out from between the hanging garments or stood howling in corners. From the cashier's desk came the words of a loud argument over the potential ownership of a sweater. And over everything hung the cloying overabundant scents of perfumes and cosmetics.

Both the noise and the smells intensified as Carol moved in among the clothing and the other shoppers. After a few moments she realized that the store was actually about average in size, but every vertical surface had been covered with mirrors.

The lack of order resolved itself. Instead of the usual divisions according to style and age appeal, Carol found that everything had been arranged item by item. Skirts hung with skirts, coats with coats, and pants with pants. For Carol this represented a surprising simplification of the shopping process. The petite, ruffled items intended for young girls, were integrated among the elegant designs intended for the older, ever dieting, fashion-conscious women.

Within a few moments Carol found three dresses. She carried them to the changing room, a large communal space where dozens of females stood in various stages of undress. Carol hung her choices on the nearest empty hook and joined the others in the business of trying on clothing.

David had better like my choice, she thought. I feel like a skinless sardine. This first one's too big. And I can tell by holding it up, that the second one will be too short. But I think this one's going to be just right.

Carol pressed a dark blue wool with a flared skirt and long sleeves against her body. Quickly she slipped it over her head. She had difficulty reaching the zipper; a woman dressed in a slip came to her assistance.

"That looks like it was made for you," observed Carol's beautifully made-up and coiffed helper. She tucked the tags into the sleeves of Carol's blue wool.

"Thanks, and thank you for the zip-up."

"Do you have your shoes with you?" Carol shook her head, no. The woman continued speaking. "When you buy a good dress you should always try it with the shoes. That way you can judge the hem and the line."

Looking at her new friend's feet Carol noticed that she wore gold lame spikes.

"For a dress like that you'll need the highest heels you can walk around on." She noticed Carol's gaze. "I don't mean anything like these," she laughed. "They would make you look like you were playing dress-up. No, for a girl your age and height, forgive me for sounding like your grandmother, but I'm guessing you're a high-school student."

"Yes, I go to West Egelton."

"My daughter goes to East. Her name is Tracy, Tracy Dodge, I don't suppose you know her?"

"No, I don't think so."

"You can recognize her by her torn, baggy blue jeans," sighed the carefully put together lady. "But that's my problem," she smiled. "Your problem is to find a pair of dark blue pumps. Shoes that will add height and a look of maturity without making you totter."

"I've never worn heels."

"Well, I'm afraid you're going to have to learn. That's the price of being a short woman with good taste. Either you walk around looking like a little girl or you give nature a boost."

Carol looked doubtful. "I'm not..."

"Believe me, without heels I look like a seven-year-old in a Halloween costume." They both laughed. "The shoe table's at the back of the store."

With great excitement Carol hurried to the jumbled pile of footwear. Finding the correct color, style, and size took some time. However, when she returned to the dressing room she was triumphant.

"Perfect," declared her advisor, who was now clothed in a shimmering, floor length evening gown.

Carol's jubilation faded when her mother insisted on inspecting the purchases. However, Mr. Clark came to his daughter's rescue by suggesting the outfit should be a surprise. He took his family out to lunch to distract them from the question of Carol's clothing.

By the time all the shopping was done and the household errands were completed, it was almost four. Barely three and a half hours, Carol realized as she lay the dark gray cardboard box on her bed. She hung the dress, clipped the tags, chose panty hose and underwear, and dusted her new shoes. Everything's going to be perfect, she thought, running her hand over the soft wool.

"Carol, come down and set the table!"

"Oh, Mom, come on, we just ate!"

"By the time supper's ready everyone'll be hungry," predicted Mrs. Clark. "So, come down and set the table."

Although she followed her mother's orders and set the table, Carol did not fall in with her prediction. She had no appetite for dinner; the food stuck in her throat.

"Stop playing with your food and eat something!" insisted her mother.

"I told you I wouldn't be hungry so soon after lunch," replied her daughter nervously.

"You have to build up your strength for your date. How about some salad?" Mr. Clark placed the wooden bowl in front of Carol's place.

"No, thank you, Daddy! I'm just not hungry."

"Well, I don't want you setting a bad example for your mother," he teased. "I think you should go upstairs right this minute!"

"May I?"

"I suppose there's no point in keeping you here," agreed her mother reluctantly.

"The sooner she dresses, the sooner we see the mystery costume." Mr. Clark gestured for Carol to leave, and she obeyed.

"I do hope she chose something appropriate."

Her mother's words echoed in the empty foyer as Carol climbed the steps.

She set up the hot rollers in her parents' bathroom. She took a quick shower and slipped on her underwear. Her anticipation grew stronger with each passing minute.

The instant, hot rollers slid easily out of Carol's short, dark curls. She grasped her mother's wood handled, natural bristle brush and attacked her unwanted ringlets. The round dressing table mirror reflected a curly headed doll in a flowered, pink organdy robe. Carol glared at herself in the brilliance of the make-up lights.

She reloaded the hotbox and waited for the indicator to light. Staring at the nautical motif on the blue and green tiled walls, Carol wondered, if I stay in here long enough, will I develop gills? She stepped closer to the dressing table; she considered the possibility that scales might be a definite improvement.

The tiny roses on the robe annoyed Carol. Her father's sister, Aunt Lou, paid for it, but Carol was sure her mother chose the robe as a gift for her fifteenth birthday last January.

Nothing looks right! How can I go on my first date looking like a misprinted Orphan Annie! Carefully handling the steaming rollers, Carol began rerolling her curls.

David's so good looking. I really want him to think I'm pretty. His smile is wonderful. I hope I can make him smile. I just love looking at him.

Her father's voice interrupted her fantasies. "Hey, Carol, you have a visitor."

"I'll be right down!" she yelled. Ignoring the heat, Carol tore the rollers free from her hair. I can't believe he's here. I must have lost all sense of time. She snatched at the robe's white, rose shaped buttons. Running through her parents' peach toned bedroom in her white cotton underwear, Carol crashed directly into Mary-Lu.

"Ouff! What's this, some kind of private marathon?" gasped her friend as she recovered her breath.

"I thought you were my date." Carol laughed with relief.

"And that's how you planned to meet him? West High's sure changed you!"

Carol pulled on her robe. "Mary-Lu, I thought . . . I mean, I haven't . . . I mean . . . oh, I've missed you." She hugged her old friend.

Mary-Lu wriggled free. "Well, Mom had to drive over here to see the dentist, something fell out and . . ." She shrugged her shoulders, "Well, you know."

"You look great." Carol noted her friend's skintight black pants and bright red shirt. "You've pierced your ears and bleached your hair."

"Blonds have more fun; you want me to do yours?"

"I don't think so, but can you flatten this frizz?" Carol led Mary-Lu into the master bedroom.

"Steam rollers, huh?"

"They're Mom's."

"You got any beer?"

"Oh, Mary-Lu!"

"For your hair! Those rollers don't work, real well, without something to help hold the curl."

Carol slid open the full-length mirror to reveal a six-foot-high, three-foot-wide cabinet lined with bottles.

"I guess this will do," said Mary-Lu, holding up a pink plastic container with a trigger spray.

Carol sat down and refilled the hot box, while Mary-Lu fumigated the room with setting lotion.

"Well," she said expectantly to Carol.

"Well, what?"

"Tell me about Prince Charming!"

"He's charming, handsome, intelligent. . . ."

"This must be your first date."

"It is."

Mary-Lu lifted out a roller and began to attach it. "With him or ever?"

Carol hesitated.

"I guess West hasn't changed you that much after all, but watch out or it will."

"What?"

"Well, you know, you've got to be real careful with guys." She finished rolling Carol's hair and squirted another layer of chemical mist. "All they want to know is how far you'll go!"

Carol forced a cough to change the subject, "Could you be more careful with that spray?"

"Close your eyes; this is the last time. Where's your hair dryer?"

"On the bottom of the cabinet."

Mary-Lu attached the cord and draped the hood over Carol's head. "You know what I mean about guys? You've got to be careful," she shouted.

Carol yelled back over the sound of the dryer. "I know what you mean, but I don't have to worry about David. He's the president of the Drama Club."

"What's that got to do with the price of beans?"

"We're starring in the fall play together."

"Starring," she found a pair of tweezers, "hey, that's nice, just like at East Junior." Before Carol could protest, Mary-Lu grabbed her chin and started changing the shape of her brows.

"That hurts!"

"But it will look great!" Mary-Lu slipped her hand under the soft, plastic bonnet. "The spray's almost dry; I'll do your make-up as soon as we disconnect you."

Carol looked up uncertainly.

"I won't do anything way out or punk; on someone your size that would look silly."

A blessing or an insult? Carol debated silently while Mary-Lu massaged in base, drew on lines, and brushed over powders.

"This make-up should last all night, if you don't get real involved, you know." She flicked off the last of a thick layer of powder.

53

Carol nodded in agreement. In spite of Mary-Lu's assurances, she tried to hold her face muscles as still as possible.

Mary-Lu's mother leaned hard on her horn. The girls rushed to wave from the bedroom window.

"Your hair won't take much messing. Wait till he rings the bell, then unroll it. Lay each piece smooth and run a brush lightly over the top."

The horn sounded again. Mary-Lu started toward the steps.

"I'll give you a call tomorrow to see how it turned out," she stopped halfway down the stairs. "And, remember, you've got to be careful!"

Carol bit her lips to stop her laughter from spoiling her make-up. She waved goodbye and returned to her room to dress.

The blue wool matched her eyes and smoothed her body into soft, graceful lines. Carol admired its simplicity with the dark blue pumps. She gloried in her new found height.

He'll be here in less than twenty minutes, less than ten minutes, less than five minutes. She counted the time while trying to master her new shoes. Carol paced in front of her closet mirror. She walked back and forth, left and right, watching her feet. As the time passed her speed increased.

She felt like she might explode. She had to do something. Carol decided to unroll her hair. Mary-Lu's miracle worked! The spray held her curls in check. Carol fashioned a smooth, sleek style according to her friend's instructions.

She stood at the mirror and brushed gently over the top of her hair to loosen the chemical stiffness. Carol found herself becoming entranced with her own image. The girl in the reflection was the girl she dreamed she might be.

Descending the stairs Carol held her body like a crystal wind chime. The hall mirror reproduced the same magic she had observed in her bedroom.

"Well, a real live princess," said her father, beaming at her reflection.

"Oh, Daddy," Carol pirouetted to face her proud father. "Do you think David will like me?"

"He'd be a fool not to, and no daughter of mine would date a fool." He winked and grinned. "You look beautiful."

"Carol, is that you?" called her mother from the kitchen. She entered the hall wearing an apron and orange rubber gloves that smelled of copper polish.

"Your hair, what have you done to it?" she demanded, descending on her daughter like a cloudburst.

Before Carol realized it, the rubber fingers broke the delicate chemical tension that held her hair in place.

"There, that's better."

"Mother!" Carol ducked, but the hall mirror showed that she was too late. "How could you do this to me!" In her anger, Carol forgot her make-up and howled with rage. "I spent hours fixing my hair and you destroyed it in five seconds!"

"But, your curls look lovely."

Carol ignored her mother while she worked on her damaged glory.

"Much nicer than that flat..."

The doorbell rang and the family froze.

"Oh, Daddy, what am I going to do?" wailed Carol.

"Smile," he suggested and opened the front door.

"Good evening, Mr. Clark?" David stepped into the hall, bringing cold air and the scent of burnt leaves with him.

"Yes, and this is my wife, Mrs. Clark." Carol noticed that her mother had managed to remove the gloves and apron.

"I believe you've met my daughter."

David's pale skin was reddened by the wind. His golden hair appeared tousled. He wore dark pants and a brightly colored Scandinavian ski sweater.

"Hi, Carol." His smile radiated warmth that melted her fears.

"I just have to get my coat."

Her mother followed her into the kitchen. "Don't you want to wear a scarf or that nice little heart locket?"

"No, thank you," she replied, taking her coat from the closet.

"That dress is so plain; I never should have let your father prevent me from helping you choose something attractive."

"Mother, I look exactly the way I want to look."

Carol returned to the hall with her mother still trailing behind her like a toddler.

"Well," said her father, "have a good time and don't stay out late!" He laughed, "I've been practicing that line all day," he confided.

Her mother broke into their laughter, "I'll be waiting for you at eleven-thirty!"

chapter
✲✲ 6 ✲✲

The door closed behind Carol and David. They walked along the flagstoned path and turned right toward town. Her heels clip-clopped on the cement. The sound echoed like gun shots in Carol's ears. She leaned forward on her toes.

What am I doing, she thought. I hardly know him. He'll think I'm crazy, tip-toeing in silence; I've got to say something.

"Nice night..." Hearing her speak, he stopped in mid-sentence.

"Beautiful evening..." Her tongue stuttered as she tried to let him continue.

They looked at each other for the first time. They both laughed.

His golden good looks thrilled her. Is this really happening to me? Carol asked herself.

"You first," he suggested.

"I was only going to say," she paused, feeling silly, "what lovely weather we seem to be having." Her sentence sounded foolish and formal to her ears.

But he responded as if she had made a brilliant observation. "Yes, I was thinking that myself."

"The air's so cool and clear," she added.

"Yes, look at the stars."

Carol was glad he did not mention Len's play. She still had not decided if she should appear as frilly, little Mandy in front of the whole school.

His long legs carried him with easy speed while she struggled to keep up. Carol thought, I don't suppose Elisha has this problem. Instead of admitting her need for slower strides, Carol asked, "What time does the film start? Are we late?"

"At eight." He checked his watch. "We have ten minutes, plenty of time."

"Yes," she agreed breathlessly.

"Am I walking too fast?" he slowed his pace. "You should have said something. I always seem to accelerate when I walk."

"I just thought it was my shoes. This is the first time I'm wearing...them." Carol caught herself mid-sentence. She had almost declared that this was the first time she had worn high heels.

"New shoes can be a problem."

As Carol and David walked down the road, they passed dozens of old two-story wooden homes. From the spacious yards came the sounds of bare tree branches cracking in the wind. Carol was glad to see the purple glow of the mercury vapor lamps at the top of the next small hill.

As they entered downtown Egelton, David said, "Your parents seem real nice."

"Yes." Pushed by the memory of her mother's recent destructive attack, Carol added, "They try very hard. And they admire your father."

"The Doctor inspires a lot of admiration."

They turned onto Center Hill Road and walked silently up to the Soda Shack. She paused in the doorway. The restaurant was empty. Later when the high-school crowds filled it, Carol hoped David and she would be among them.

"Come on, Carol. It's getting late," he called to her from the shadows three doorways ahead.

She clattered along hurrying to catch up with him. He reached the theatre a few moments ahead of her. When she arrived at the ticked window, he was fumbling with his change and making a very slow and elaborate business of replacing his wallet.

He stared into the empty lobby and began to move. "Hey," David called over his shoulder, urging Carol across the florescent lit space, "I don't want to miss the beginning."

She tripped on the worn red carpeting. He half caught, half dragged her. They pushed through the padded double doors and stood still in the cool, smoky auditorium.

A short film about a lush, tropical island shed too little light for them to find seats. After a few minutes David grasped Carol's forearm and pulled her up the stairs to the balcony.

Carol felt her heartbeat race faster with each step. The balcony, she thought, I've never sat in the balcony. It's so romantic.

She could barely see David's tall, silhouette, but the warmth of his grip radiated through her body. Carol was disappointed to find that when she sat down, he released his hold.

Carol looked up expecting David to settle in the seat beside her. But he continued to stand. He seemed to be watching or waiting for something.

"I'm going to get some popcorn; do you want yours with butter?"

"Sure."

After he left, Carol realized that they were seated in a smoking section. Her eyes felt dry. No one in her family used tobacco. She wondered if David smoked. She'd never seen him with a cigarette.

He returned just as *Citizen Kane* started.

"Thank you, but I can't eat all that," whispered Carol,

accepting a giant-sized container of buttered popcorn.

"Try your best, I have great faith in you." He sat beside her with his own equally oversized portion.

Words flashed on the screen. "In Xanadu did Kubla Khan a mighty pleasure dome decree..."

"That's by the poet Coleridge," Carol murmured, surprised that freshman English applied to real life.

"Shhh, watch carefully; the beginning's real important."

Carol waited quietly through the opening but when the film flashed back to Kane's early life, she asked, "David, do you smoke?"

"Of course not! Now, shhh! This is the big scene."

The child Kane would inherit some money and had to live with his benefactor. Carol agreed that he seemed to need it, but she wondered why David thought this particular scene was so important.

Repeatedly blinking her eyes to soften the effect of the smoke, she whispered, "Can we move downstairs?"

"These seats have the best view." David answered without looking at Carol.

She found that watching David's profile was more exciting than the black and white film. But he seemed to have entirely forgotten her existence and their date. From time to time she noticed his eyes left the screen to scan the audience. She wondered if as an actress she too should be studying the audience.

Carol found herself swallowing the popcorn with increasing rapidity. Excitement prevented her from eating much dinner. Now, with David's attention elsewhere, she felt hungry. At first, Carol worried that David might not want to hold her buttery hand. Then she realized his hands would also be greased. But the longer she sat there watching him divide his interest between the orchestra and the film, the more she realized the problem would never arise. So much for the wisdom and experience of Mary-Lu, Carol thought with disappointment.

Kane's empire rose. Carol began to cough. She tried to hold it back. She didn't want to bother David; but the more she tried to restrain it, the more she sputtered and choked from the foul air.

David pounded her back, "Too much popcorn; I'll get you a soda."

"No," she gasped, "it's the smoke!—"

"I'll be right back, hold my seat!" He cut off her second request to move before she could make it.

By the time he returned, the coughing fit had passed.

"Here, this will help!"

The cola burned her already irritated throat. "Thanks, but . . ."

"Watch! Elisha said the next part's really funny."

"Elisha?"

"She was by the candy stand."

Carol heard the audience laugh, but her attention had wandered away from the movie. *While she was choking David had taken time to chat with Elisha? I suppose he had to say something to her. He's very polite.* Carol smiled at the profile of her golden-haired date.

Sucking on the ice felt better than drinking the bubbling soda. But when it all melted the feeling of dryness returned. She suffered in silence until the discomfort became overpowering.

"David, please," Carol whispered, "let's move downstairs."

"It's almost over; we'll run right outside," he promised, keeping his eyes on the screen.

Sipping at the warm cola and taking shallow breaths, Carol waited for the film to end.

The moment the credits flashed, David stood up and took Carol's arm.

61

"Come on, let's get you out of here."

He almost lifted her off her feet. Carol was glad that her two-and-a-half-inch heels made it possible for them to walk arm in arm.

The sudden light in the lobby dazzled her. David jerked her across the room. They moved out to Center Hill Road and turned on a shadowy side street so quickly that Carol's eyes did not need to adjust.

"I'm sorry the smoke bothered you." David released her arm and paused. "Maybe you should do some deep breathing to clear your lungs."

"I'm fine now." Carol wanted to reassure him. She felt flattered that he had hurried her into the fresh air with so much show of concern. "It mostly bothered my eyes."

"Your eyes! You should have said something. The reason I sat up there was to see better. *Citizen Kane* is visually a very important film."

They ambled along the block of darkened store fronts. While they passed a dry cleaners, a junk shop, and a plumber's office, he lectured her on the merits of the movie.

"The director, Orson Welles, invented all those weird, eerie shots." David started to cut across a poorly lighted parking lot. "Before Welles made *Citizen Kane,* most . . ."

Carol interrupted his speech, "Where are we going?"

"It's only a little after ten. I thought you might like a soda or something."

She nodded and thought, we're walking in the wrong direction! The Soda Shack is on the other side of the theatre.

"There's a place over there on the far side . . . we could walk all the way around the block, but this is faster."

Carol followed David across the seemingly abandoned

open space. She silently picked her way with care through the potholes and litter.

They skirted the trash barrels to reach the back entrance of an old wood building. A bare bulb illuminated the peeling brown paint.

David held open the wooden frame of a sagging screen door. Carol pushed at the metal fire door. After the windy darkness, the heat, noise, and smells of the restaurant nearly overpowered her.

If David had not pushed her forward, Carol would have bolted out the door. No one was in the room to notice their entrance.

David pointed to a dimly lit hallway. Carol accepted his direction. But her eyes needed time to readjust. She placed her hand on the imitation wood paneling and used the wall to guide her past the restrooms.

The hall ended in a game room where half a dozen video and several traditional pinball machines whirred, beeped, bonged, and sent up technicolor displays. The air smelled like stale beer and cigarette butts.

Even in the dim light Carol could see the players were kids. They wore leather and denim and used curse words for punctuation.

David had already passed through the swinging door into the restaurant, when Carol heard her name.

"Carol, what's a nice girl like you doing in a place like this!" Mary-Lu bounded out from the shadows.

"Where am I?"

"The Corner Bar. Where's Prince Charming?"

"I was just following him," Carol looked for David, but he had vanished.

"You snuck in the back way?"

"Help me find him and I'll introduce you." The girls walked into the restaurant.

The vinyl padded bar stretched almost the entire length of the room. A mirror covered the wall behind the bottles.

Carol stared in dismay at the shattered remnants of her hairdo.

"Your makeup still looks good; that spray didn't hold real well," commented Mary-Lu, observing her friend's distress.

Carol quickly searched the room and changed the subject. "There he is, over on the end." She pointed to the booth farthest from the door.

"He seems to like privacy," cracked Mary-Lu as they approached the formica topped table. "He's as good looking as you promised."

"David, I'd like you to meet my friend, Mary-Lu."

He barely looked up. He mumbled something that might have been hello into the stained and burnt table.

The girls stood in awkward silence.

"I guess you two want to be alone. I have to get back to my asteroids, anyway!" Mary-Lu backed away from the table.

"How do you know her?" David demanded as Carol slid onto the bench opposite his.

"Mary-Lu was my best friend at East Junior. I don't see her much anymore."

"Oh, she goes to East," he said as if that made her human. He checked his watch. "We don't have a lot of time."

"The kitchen clock said ten. I don't have to be home until eleven-thirty."

"You can't trust bar clocks."

Carol smiled at this bit of sophisticated knowledge. She wondered how many bars David had visited. "Do they have a menu?"

"Yeah, but they're usually all greasy." He laughed.

"I think I'll have some orange juice."

David waved at the bartender, who shouted, "What d' ya' want?"

"An orange juice and a cola."

"Heavy drinkers," he laughed as he set the glasses on the bar for David to pick up. "No table service till after eleven!"

Carol watched David walk across and realized that this front room was almost empty.

"Here you go, down the hatch." David seemed to drink his soda in one gulp.

Carol hesitated over her juice.

"Don't you want it?"

"Yes, but the glass has lipstick stains."

David checked his watch, "Well, we're each supposed to eat a peck of dirt in a lifetime."

"I don't think I want it."

"Okay, I'll walk you home." He stood and strode to the door before Carol could slide off her bench.

She walked as quickly as her high heels would permit. "Wait, please." She caught him on the street. They stood in front of the red neon sign that flashed *Corner Bar and Restaurant*.

"David, is anything wrong? Did I say something . . . ?"

"No!" He checked his watch again. "It's time to walk you home. I wouldn't want your parents to worry or anything."

It seemed to Carol that she had never moved so fast. Yet, the silent five minute walk took forever. When they finally reached the house, David stopped at the flagstone path. He did not even accompany her to the door. He just turned and would have left without a word except that Carol called to him.

"David, what time is it?"

"Ten-thirty," he shouted over his shoulder almost running along the suburban street.

Carol opened the front door and found her mother standing in the foyer.

"Very good, you're home on time."

"I'm home early," replied her daughter rushing up the stairs and into the privacy of her pink and white ruffled bedroom.

chapter
⋆⋆ 7 ⋆⋆

"But you can't drop out!" Len's frustration propelled his body to heights that mere potholes had never achieved.

Carol slumped into their bus seat like a bundle of wet wash. "Today's only the first rehearsal, you can still choose someone else."

The bus splattered great gushes of October rain from the puddled streets. Mud spots made the windows opaque. The wetness dampened the usual morning noise.

Len was able to use intensity, rather than volume, to make his points. "I don't want to choose anyone else! You gave the best audition I ever saw. You're the best actress West Egelton High's ever had!"

"You're just saying that because I look the part."

"Look the part! Of course you look the part. Everyone in the cast looks their parts." He changed his voice to an imitation of W.C. Fields. "That's why we use girls for the girls' parts and boys for the boys' parts, my little Chickadee."

Carol ignored his clowning. "Elisha said that's the only reason you chose me."

"That's ridiculous, there are dozens of girls who could look like Mandy! In fact," he smiled wickedly and wiggled his eyebrows. "Almost any girl, except Elisha."

"But she said you were ready to use a junior-high student."

"If you listen to that peroxide dodo, you deserve what

you hear!" Len exclaimed with exasperation. "She's just jealous. Elisha thinks she's the club goddess, and we lowly members should worship at her size twelve feet!"

"Size twelve?" Carol squirmed around in her seat to get the view down the aisle. As usual, Elisha's long legs sprawled into the middle of the bus.

"Yeah, I heard her making a fuss about how she hates buying shoes."

"That doesn't matter," Carol looked at her reflection in the darkened window. "I still don't want to do the show."

"Why not?"

"I can't explain it!"

"I bet you can."

"I don't want to."

"Not even to poor old Uncle Len?" He hunched over and managed to look like a wizzened gnome.

In spite of her misery, Carol found herself smiling.

"It's about time, next I was going to tear off your shoes and tickle your feet."

"Len, I don't want to disappoint you. But I can't be in your play. Elisha hates me and David won't speak to me." Carol covered her mouth with her right hand, as if to keep the words from escaping. She had not intended to mention David. She had been so busy concentrating on hiding her fears about appearing as frilly, little Mandy, that the results of her unhappy Saturday night slipped out before she could stop it.

"David won't speak to you?"

"We had a date this weekend," she admitted.

"Ah, ha!"

"It was awful," Carol sighed. "I can't even talk about it."

Len put on a mock German accent, "Ve have our vays to make you talk!"

68

"It was terrible; it was probably all my own fault, anyway. I thought it was going to be so wonderful, and everything I did seemed to be wrong." Carol paused as the memories flooded her consciousness.

"Where did you go?" Len prompted softly.

Carol responded as if she were hypnotized. "We went to the movies."

"And..."

. "We went to see *Citizen Kane*, and he wanted to sit in the balcony. We did sit in the balcony; but it was a smoking section and I felt awful. He didn't understand. Then I started to cough, and I couldn't see the film..." Carol's fast accelerating flood of words stopped at Len's interruption.

"Wait, my ears can only receive at thirty-three and a third RPM!"

Carol remembered Len's previous instructions. She took a deep breath and let it out slowly. "David took me to the movie, and afterwards we went to the Corner Bar. Then suddenly he got all moody and stopped talking."

"Why the Corner? Do you like that place?"

"My old friend from East Junior, Mary-Lu, hangs out there, but I'd never been inside it before," Carol wrinkled her nose with displeasure. "David chose it. He made me walk through a deserted parking lot to get there!" She added with indignation.

"Did you by any chance just happen to notice any sign of Elisha?"

"David said she was in the theatre, but I didn't see her."

"Ah, ha, the plot thickens. I believe," Len patted Carol's cheek, "my dear, you have been the innocent victim of a classic love triangle."

"A what?" She gently batted his hand away.

The bus stopped. Rain played a tattoo on the metal

69

roof. Students moved reluctantly toward the doors.

"David and Elisha, they're like that self-reversing magnet in the science display. They're attracted to each other until they get too close; then suddenly boom! They blow apart, trailing every iron filing in the place after them."

Carol gathered her still damp books and started for the exit. She spoke over her shoulder, "I don't think I like being called an iron filing."

Len moved close behind her and whispered into Carol's ear, "It's the official, secret Drama Club initiation!" The line paused. He glanced around, and then spoke in a normal voice. "She can be vicious, but I don't think he realizes the trouble he causes."

They reached the wet sidewalk and Len yelled over the sound of rushing water. "I predict David will apologize before lunch!"

As they ran toward the nearest entrance, Carol shouted, "I'm still not sure I can do the show."

"I'll see you later at rehearsal." Len vanished into the crowd.

Carol shook the water from her matted curls. Miniature streams ran down the decorative details of her pink plastic raincoat. She had wanted a trench coat, but her mother refused to spend what she called "that kind of money" for an occasional garment. Especially for one that she thought of as dull and unattractive.

The first bell sounded. Carol realized that the rain must have delayed the bus. She hurried into the lobby and around the corner of the auditorium. In her rush, Carol passed the drama office and the club bulletin board without noticing them.

Suddenly a hand grabbed her shoulder from behind. It was so unexpected, that she tried to keep walking like a character in an animated cartoon.

"I know you're angry. But at least you could let me apologize."

Startled, Carol stopped moving and looked up into the clear, emerald green of David's eyes. Her pulse jumped. In spite of everything, Carol found herself responding to his touch. She wanted him to slide his arm around her. For a moment Carol imagined what it would be like to have him make that casual gesture; the one that would tell the whole school she was his girl.

"I really am sorry. I know Saturday night was terrible. It was all Elisha's fault, I . . ."

At the mention of Elisha's name, Carol stiffened and pulled away. "I'll be late; I can't talk." She started running toward her homeroom.

David's long legs kept easy pace with her attempt at speed. "Look, you have every right to be mad; I just want a chance to explain."

Carol grabbed at the doorknob. David put his hand over hers. He held the door closed, making a sandwich of her hand between his and the knob. His strength both thrilled and annoyed her.

"Say you'll sit with me at lunch, and I'll let you go."

"All right, anything, I just don't . . ."

The bell rang; David released her hand.

". . . want to be late." Carol finished her sentence in a defeated tone.

As she pushed open the door, David said, "I'll meet you at the water cooler by the windows."

"A tryst, Miss Clark?" asked Mr. Brockton. His voice boomed in the silence that followed the bell.

"No! I mean . . ." Carol hugged her books and felt a riverlet of water slide off her slicker and onto her left shoe.

"No need to explain, just take your seat."

Her wet shoe made a squishing sound, and the plastic

71

coat squeaked against the polished plywood seat.

"This is your third demerit."

"It can't be," Carol responded aloud without thinking.

"The printout indicates you received two last week; apparently both on the same day."

"But, David..." She let the sentence trail off. He promised, Carol thought; it's not fair. How could David do this to me?

"You have something to tell the class, Miss Clark?"

Carol just shook her head.

"In that case, you will be expected in 729, the detention room, at two-thirty."

"But, I can't."

"I'm afraid you'll have to. You can discuss your problem at two thirty. Vice-Principal Bradly will be waiting in room 729. For the rest of you, there will be a meeting of the Romantic Literature Club in room..."

Carol ignored the announcements while she considered her problems. Maybe, if I promise to take detention some other day, Vice Principal Bradly will let me go to the rehearsal. It's the first one; he has to understand how important that is...

Of course, if I drop out of the show...but I can't drop out without upsetting Len. I don't want to hurt him; he's been so very nice to me. I really like him, but that's no reason to act in his play if it makes me uncomfortable.

But even if I do drop out, I should go to the rehearsal to tell them. Except that I have to go to detention. If only David had sent that pass; he said he would.

I never should have trusted him. I never should have gone out with him. I knew it was too good to be true when he asked me to go to the movies.

Why am I having lunch with him? I should be furious with David. He caused all my problems! If only he had taken care of the pass; if only he hadn't acted so strange

72

on Saturday night; if only he hadn't delayed me in the hall this morning; if only he liked me more than Elisha.

The circle of thoughts continued to rotate through Carol's mind. When the bell rang, she ran to her locker. She hung up the now dry raincoat and exchanged the books she used at home for those she needed in class.

Her song of extracurricular misery stopped mid-note. Carol frantically emptied her locker. Her French text had vanished. She remembered holding it on the bus, but now it was gone. Leaving the locker standing open, she hurried across the hall to her homeroom. There was no sign of the book.

She tossed everything back into the locker and ran as fast as she could to her first class, Dr. Edwards', history.

If she appeared in French without her text, Carol knew Madame Schutz would mark her zero for the day. Carol usually received good grades. She had never had a zero in any class. A zero and a fourth demerit for lateness was more than Carol could bear to think about. She forced her feet to move as quickly as possible.

She arrived just as the bell sounded. None of the other students were at their desks, either. No one noticed her late entrance. Carol dropped her books on the formica top and collapsed into the attached chair.

After a moment, as her breathing evened, she realized that the seeming chaos had an order. Students were handing in their monthly history reports.

Hers, titled The American Theatre During the Civil War, came to five typed pages. Carol had enjoyed the research. She was glad Dr. Edwards had allowed her to choose her own topic this time. However, she hated the typing. With her two-fingered approach on her mother's old, manual machine, it had taken her all day on Sunday to complete the paper.

She opened her loose-leaf notebook and let out a little

scream of dismay. The rain had soaked the edge of the blue cardboard cover. Purplish stains streaked her neatly typed pages. In several places the words had become unintelligible. When Carol tried to separate the damp pages, they stuck together and disintegrated into lumps.

Carol felt the tears well up and over. Just more water she thought, and made no effort to stop the tears from rolling down her face or splattering on the already spoiled pages.

She was aware that Dr. Edwards stood at her desk looking down at the mess that had been her report.

"Carol, it's all right." The teacher tried to reassure her with her clipped, almost British speech.

Carol looked up, but did not feel she could say anything. She handed Dr. Edwards her soggy folder.

She waved it away. "I see that you brought the report in on time. I'll make it present. All you need to do is go home, retype it, and bring it back tomorrow. You won't lose any credit."

Carol received the expected zero from Madame Schutz for her missing French text book. Her other classes were uneventful. In fact, the morning seemed to drag while Carol waited for lunch period. After careful consideration, she had decided to tell David about her detention, and how she felt it was his fault. First, he neglected to send the pass as he had promised, and, second, he had detained her in the hall. Carol believed that David's response would help her determine whether or not she would be able to act in Len's play.

The cafeteria was almost empty when she arrived. Carol stood by the water cooler at the windows and watched the pale, green tiled room fill with students.

She waved to the table of sophomore girls she usually sat with at lunch. Carol tried to imagine their conversation and speculations when handsome David White

74

greeted her and they went off together. She had told them about his asking her out for a date. Carol knew they were waiting for a report on how it went.

Fifteen minutes after the bell, Carol was still standing at the water cooler. When she finally saw David coming toward her, Elisha was at his side.

Carol's anger bubbled over like water from a clogged fountain. She could not tell if they had noticed her standing like a statue by a pool, but Carol decided that she was not about to wait for him and his, what had Len called her, his peroxide dodo, to further embarrass her!

She rushed into the girl's room, locked herself in a stall, and sat down to remove her wet socks. Carol stayed in the compartment quietly reading the graffiti, while the other girls came and went. Finally she lined her shoes with tissue paper to protect her bare feet and left the booth.

She had finished rinsing her socks and was rolling them in a paper towel, when Elisha sailed into the pink and gray room. She wore a calf-length, red, skirt with a matching vest and flimsy white blouse.

"Ah, Miss Muffet, I see you're representing the new, revised Mother Goose, curds and socks!" Elisha opened a plastic case filled with cosmetics. She laid out her tools in battle formation on the shelf above the sink.

Carol did not know how to answer, but she refused to be intimidated. She finished wrapping the socks and put them in her bag. Then she went to the sink next to Elisha's to wash her face.

When Carol finished drying herself, Elisha caught her eyes in the mirror. "Did you enjoy the symbolic imagery of *Citizen Kane,* or were you too busy hiding your date in the smoke?"

Carol just returned Elisha's stare with what she hoped was a look of weary indifference. She gathered her books and left the room without a word. Carol could hear Elisha's laughter echoing on the tiled walls. She thought, I know that I'll find the perfect answer for that sometime next week. There probably isn't any symbolism in *Citizen Kane*.

Lunch period was almost over. The noise and activity had reached their maximum possible level. Carol glanced toward the food counters, but nothing appealed to her. Her appetite had subsided with the day's disasters.

David was nowhere to be seen, but Carol knew he no longer mattered. Elisha's nastiness had convinced her to perform in the show. Len's right, and if just my presence bothers her that much, I'm going to act her off the stage and drive her crazy! She'll hate that more than any . . .

Len interrupted Carol's plan of revenge. "I've been all over the school trying to find you! Here!" He held out her missing French text. "I hope you didn't need it."

"Did I leave it on the bus?"

"No, it must have slipped in with my pile. I didn't find it till second period was ending, and I went to pack up my books."

Carol noticed that Len's black turtleneck was torn on the shoulder seam.

"Thanks, Len, it's real nice of you to be concerned." She looked down and saw that in spite of the rain, Len's shoes shone from careful waxing. His clothing always puzzled Carol.

"I have to protect my interests; after all, you are still my star!"

"You were right, David apologized, and I've decided that I shall appear in your play!" She tried to sound as if she were putting on a sophisticated act. Carol didn't want to say anything about her new reasons for acting in the club show.

Len took a dramatic pose, placing his left hand on his

hip while flinging his right across his heart. "A true actress can never resist a really well-written part."

"I suppose not," she hesitated, "but, I have a problem . . . I'm scheduled for detention today."

"For shame!" Len clicked his tongue. "Stealing erasers, huh?"

"This is serious. I'm going to miss the rehearsal!"

"I assume you are a first time offender," he paused and looked more amused than worried.

"It's your show; if you don't care, I suppose it . . ."

"Don't get angry! I'm only teasing you. First time detention is only twenty minutes. You'll be in the auditorium before we begin the reading."

"Really!" she squealed.

"Any other problems, Dr. Leonard Fixit to the rescue with a hardy hi! ho! hummm—there's the bell. Which way are you walking?"

"Downstairs to the library."

"Too bad my presence is required in the east wing."

"Do you mean the big gym?"

"I never use that sort of vulgarity. Now, I really must be going!" He left her standing at the head of the stairs.

A small blister on Carol's left foot was the biggest problem she encountered after lunch. Just as Len said, Vice-Principal Bradly kept her only twenty minutes. And she reached the rehearsal before the start of the reading.

David cornered her at the back of the auditorium. "I've been waiting for you! Now it's you who owes me an apology."

Carol refused to look at him. She now knew herself well enough to avoid David's obvious attractiveness. "David, leave me alone!" She tried to dart away from him like a basketball forward dodging a guard.

"Not until you tell me why you ran away in the cafeteria." He stepped in front of her and trapped her between the wall and his outstretched arms.

Carol fought her fantasy of David sweeping her into his embrace. "I didn't think we'd make a happy couple, you, Elisha and me!"

"If you'd waited, I could have explained everything."

"You don't owe me any explanation. Just leave me alone. Everytime you come around I get into trouble."

"All right," he held up his hands in a signal of surrender, "Saturday night was bad, but trouble? Isn't that a little harsh?"

"I just came from detention because you didn't send the pass last week, and you kept me out in the hall this morning." Carol's words hissed like a snake getting ready to strike.

"You're right, I forgot about the pass, but it's your own fault. I was so pleased, because you said you'd go out with me."

"Oh, come on . . ."

"All right, I'm sorry! I'm really sorry, but if you'd waited at lunch, I could . . ."

"I know," she interrupted, "explained everything. Why don't you just do it now and get it over with?"

"It's a long story."

"How about the abridged edition?"

"Okay, I used to go with Elisha, now we've broken up!"

"I understand this is a twice-told tale."

"You're right, we have broken up before, but this time it's really over, for good, totally finished." He gave Carol one of his best sunshine and dimples smiles. "That's what we were saying in the cafeteria. I just wish you had waited."

"If I had waited, I suppose we would have had to eat under one of the tables, so your ex-girlfriend wouldn't have noticed!"

"Look, I already apologized for Saturday night. I've admitted I was trying to avoid Elisha. But that's done, gone, no more! Here, I'll prove it to you. I'd like you to be my date at the Drama Club's Thanksgiving party. Everybody will be there. We'll be right out in the open."

"Everyone on stage with scripts, right now!" called Nancy Rodgers.

"I don't know."

Carol started down the aisle. David stuck to her side.

"Please, look, you owe me something for standing me up at lunch."

"I'll think about it!"

"It's always a nice party. Val's parents give it every year on the first Friday of Thanksgiving vacation."

"I said I'd think about it!" Carol snapped. She crossed the circle of chairs and seated herself between Peggy and Maris from her English class.

"Don't you want to sit next to David?" whispered Peggy.

"There are two free seats across the way," observed Maris.

"Too late, Elisha's snagged him, again," sighed Peggy.

"Oh, come on, you two, stop acting like he's some kind of combination between Prince Charming and the Fonz." In her mind Carol added, maybe I should say, come on, we three.

chapter
⋆⋆⋆ 8 ⋆⋆⋆

As they left her front steps, the crunch and squeak of sand and ice under Carol's feet distracted her from David's attempt to make conversation.

"Don't you agree?" he insisted for the second time.

Her blue pumps wobbled slightly as she tried to step around a dangerously slippery patch on the flagstone walk.

David quickly slipped his right hand under Carol's left arm. "Better let me help you. Everything's frozen up again."

Carol was glad he had forgotten the question she had missed hearing. She was reminded of their first disastrous date as she replied, "Today's sunshine was just too good to last."

"Yes," he mumbled, as he guided her around the snowdrift covered lawn and up the driveway. He treated Carol as if she were as fragile as the fan of silver threaded icicles that curtained her bedroom windows.

She delighted in his courtesy. Even though she saw David everyday at the after school rehearsals, they had not spoken privately since he asked her to be his date for the Thanksgiving party. Carol had noticed that he still seemed very friendly with Elisha. She was surprised when David phoned her at the beginning of the week to reissue the party invitation. David seemed so sincere in his desire for her company that she agreed to go with him.

He saved her from a sudden slide across the frozen topped cement. "Why do you wear those dumb shoes?"

Feeling the pressure of his grip on her upper arm, Carol thought, if I didn't, you'd have to walk on your knees to hold me that way. But she recognized that a person David's height would be puzzled by that sort of reply. Instead, she answered in a mock southern drawl. "I had no idea you disliked them."

"They look okay; everything you're wearing, your whole . . . you know . . ." He searched for the word. "Outfit," he said triumphantly, "looks great. But those high heels are dangerous, especially on snow like this."

A warm flush added color to the pink of Carol's already wind-burned cheeks. She had had to argue long and hard with her mother to wear the clothes she had chosen. Mrs. Clark's disapproval of her daughter's simple dress for her last date had made her wary about letting Carol dress herself for this one. But Carol had exerted her best arguments and now wore her blue and green, V-necked jumper without its frilly, pink blouse. She believed the unadorned wool looked chic and sophisticated with her dark, blue heels. Carol was delighted to hear that her glamorous date appreciated her efforts.

"Thank you, David. I think you look real nice, too."

He wore the dark slacks and Scandinavian, multicolored, pullover that he had worn on their ill-fated evening at the movies. Only now he had exchanged his loafers for water proof work boots and added a forest green down vest over the sweater.

His golden curls gleamed in the moonlight. Carol watched as their combined breath formed vapor clouds. She imagined him climbing a mountain, or as an advertisement for a Norwegian airline. It's really unfair for a boy to be so good looking, she thought.

David helped her into a white compact with red vinyl

seats. He adjusted her shoulder harness and closed the door. Carol inhaled the lingering new car fragrance, while he hurried around to the driver's side and seated himself.

A fast talking AM rock and roll station came on when he turned the ignition key. The announcer pitched a skin care product, some salad dressings, and told them they could expect to be very cold; all before David could pull out of Carol's driveway.

"It's a nice car," she shouted over the patter and engine noise.

"Yeah, my parents bought it for my sister when she graduated."

The radio played the old Rolling Stone's "I Can't Get No Satisfaction."

"Will they buy one for you?"

"I think so, but it depends on what college I get into. My sister commutes to State."

"Is that where you want to go?"

David launched into a complex lecture about board scores, class place, and applications. Although Carol realized she would eventually need to know these things, for the moment she equated them with her understanding of football; the idea is to win. With colleges winning means going to your first choice school.

Remembering the awkward conversation that began their last date, Carol decided to hide her ignorance and let David ramble through his monologue.

Outside the car windows Egelton prepared for a traditional New England Christmas. The radio's music clashed with the frosted countryside. Carol watched as the brick and shingled homes gave way to sprawling farms and occasional grand Victorian mansions with snow-trimmed gingerbread decorations. She would have gladly traded Joan Jett, AC/DC, and the GoGo's for one softly harmonized holiday song.

"Does Val live on a farm?"

"Her folks have an old farm house with a few acres around it. They've had the club out for a spring picnic and fall party every year since Val's older sister was a member."

"Do they grow anything?"

"Yeah, but only for themselves; they're into the back-to-the-land thing."

"That's interesting, I'd never have guessed it from the cola and potato-chip snacks Val munches through every rehearsal."

"I don't think she's allowed any of that stuff at home."

"What about us?" Carol asked, wondering about the food at the party.

"Not to worry! Most of us have learned to bring things. Look in the back seat."

While Carol loosened her seatbelt to turn around, David eased her fears, "Val's Mom is a good cook, even if they eat strange stuff. Last year she made something out of soybeans and seaweed! And it was good!"

Carol laughed and stretched to see the shopping bags overflowing with plastic packed junk foods. "You must have broken your piggy bank."

"The Club pays for them."

The engine coughed and stopped. The car coasted to the sound of "Whip It." David guided it to the side of the road.

"Nuts!"

"What's wrong?"

"We're out of gas!"

"You're kidding, that's out of an old joke."

"Only after the party, but by then I'll be rushing home to murder Susan!"

"Is that your sister's name?"

"Yeah, she said the tank was low, not empty."

"You mean, you knew and didn't do anything about it?" Carol made no effort to keep the astonishment out of her voice.

"Why should I put my money into her car?"

Carol shook her head as if to clear her ears of disbelief and to refuse the possibility that her glamorous, golden date could have said such a thing.

The moonlight reflected on the rolling hills of snow. Dark, shadowy trees stretched upward like empty hands. Beautiful, quiet, and deserted, the land offered no suggestion of assistance. No cars passed.

After a few moments, Carol ventured, "I don't think I've seen any open service stations since we left town."

"That's okay. My family belongs to an auto club. They'll bring us some gas. All I need is to find a telephone." David unbuckled his safety belt. "I guess I'm going to have to walk; there don't seem to be any cars out tonight."

"Everyone's probably home with their TV sets; the radio said it would be very cold."

"Thanks for reminding me!" he said with annoyance.

She recoiled slightly and stammered, "I didn't...I mean...I mean that if we walked to the next house, someone will probably be home."

"Do you think you can walk anywhere in those shoes?"

"I guess not."

"That's okay," David replied as if he were granting her a big favor. "I'll go. You stay here; at least the car's warm and the radio still works."

He stepped onto the road and slammed the door.

Almost as soon as it closed Carol turned off the radio. A light snow began to fall and the absolute silence soothed her anger.

Because David had picked her up late, she had had to spend an extra forty-five minutes fending off her mother's attempts to change and accessorize her outfit. Carol had been worried about arriving at the party late. Now they would be even later.

Len had offered her a ride. He and a carload of other kids had volunteered to go out early and help Val to set up. He made it sound like a lot of fun. But she had already accepted David White's invitation.

When Carol told Len that she would be going as David's date, Len had stopped talking and just stared at her. Finally he spoke, "Some people never learn."

Carol had not known what to say. Now she wished she had some excuse to offer, for her own as well as for Len's benefit.

A yellow pickup truck pulled up behind the compact. A middle-aged man in a red parka climbed out of the driver's side. David balanced an emergency fuel can and swung out of the passenger seat. Neither male spoke to Carol nor made any sign to indicate that her presence had been observed.

They poured the gas into the tank and exchanged a few words. The older man took the empty can and left. David stormed into the car.

He flipped on the radio and fastened his seatbelt. "Whew, I thought the battery must have died."

"Looks like we were really lucky! An auto club can take forever to arrive."

"Lucky! He charged me almost double for that gallon!"

Carol let the radio do the talking for her. "Enough is enough is enough" sang the seemingly endless old disco song. She thought, it's the first appropriate bit of music that we've heard since we entered this car.

The remainder of the trip took less time than the fuel search. Carol wondered if she had known, would she have walked to Val's in spite of her shoes?

Val's floodlit yard looked like a highway during a holiday rush hour. Cars of all sizes, shapes, and conditions stood abandoned without pattern or plan.

David carefully parked his sister's compact at a distance from the haphazard mess. "Don't want any problems when we want to leave."

He leaped from the driver's seat and rushed to open Carol's door. "Guess I'll have to help you up this drive." Without another word, he reached in behind Carol and scooped her up like a child.

She sputtered like the car engine. "Put me down!"

"Stop wiggling!"

"David, I don't want to be carried!"

"The dirt's all rutted; you'll never make it to the house."

All Carol's tender romantic dreams were being crushed like a sack of potatoes. "I can walk by myself!"

She gave a great kick.

"Now you've done it!" David yelled in her ear as he slowly lost his balance and toppled sideways taking Carol with him.

Carol felt as if they were suspended in time. The fall lasted far longer than the laws of gravity should permit. A feeling of nausea rose from her stomach to her throat. It stifled her would-be screams.

When they finally bounced on the frost hardened ground of the mud drive, Carol heard the tinkling of cracking ice followed by a great cheer. She looked up, too startled to feel any pain from her fall.

The entire drama club, plus a few guests and relations, stood on Val's wide wooden porch. Some held paper plates or plastic glasses. Everyone was laughing.

Carol felt anger and embarrassment rush through her like a raging fire. She felt her cheeks burn red. She believed this was the worst thing David had done to her. Carol felt like a fool. She listened to the other kids laugh.

She thought, no matter how dumb I feel, they probably think I look even dumber!

Before she could rise or speak, Len was by her side. He held her left pump in his hand.

Carol looked at the shoe and then at her feet. Until that moment she had not noticed that her left foot was bare. She realized that the shoe must have flown off during her kick for freedom.

"Well, Princess, you certainly know how to make an entrance." Len slipped the leather pump into place and pulled Carol to her feet. "Nothing broken I trust."

Quickly, assessing that nothing more than her pride seemed damaged, Carol dusted herself off and turned toward the house.

The other students continued to laugh and yell from the porch. Someone started chanting the silly cheer from Len's play. "Sis! Boom! Bee! Kick him in the knee! Sis! Boom! Bah! Kick him in the other knee!" The whole group repeated it several times with unbridled enthusiasm.

Carol cringed and blushed, still deeper, with each repetition. She refused to even look at David. She sincerely hoped that his ego was not his only bruised part.

She started marching toward the wooden steps. But Carol was surprised and annoyed to find David had been right. The ice glazed peaks and valleys of the frozen dirt drive threatened her ankles at every step. She struggled forward, slipping and wobbling on her high heels.

Len stepped in front of her almost causing Carol to take a second fall. As she swayed to regain her balance, he made an elaborate bow with extended flourishes of his nonexistant hat. "Would you permit me the honor of escorting you to the punch bowl?"

Their audience whooped with glee on the word "punch." Carol tried to ignore them. Len waved his make-believe hat and gave them a quick bow.

Holding her head high and her hands out for balance, Carol carefully stepped around Len and picked her unsteady way toward the porch. When he caught up to her, Carol glared at Len for increasing her embarrassment when all she wanted was to disappear.

The round of applause that greeted Carol's successful arrival at the wooden steps was cut short by Val's mother. She slipped her arm around Carol's waist and guided her into the house. "I thought it suddenly got awfully quiet in the living room." She motioned at the others with her free hand, "The show's over; everyone get back inside."

Carol found herself sitting by a woodburning stove in an old-fashioned, country farm kitchen. Plants, dry leaves, and gadgets hung in charming disarray from the beamed ceiling. Patchwork pillows softened the hand-carved bench where she sat.

"Here, this should warm you right up."

Carol gratefully sipped at the hot, sweet drink. It tasted of apples. A stick of cinnamon and some cloves floated in her mug.

"Thank you, this was just what I needed; what is it?"

"It's called mulled cider. We drink it a lot during the cold months." She, too, drank a mug of the hot beverage. "We haven't met yet. I'm Val's mother; the club members call me Mrs. R."

Carol noticed that this small, redheaded woman, looked very much like her daughter.

"I'm Carol Clark."

"Val says you won the part of Mandy right out from under her."

Carol hesitated, uncertain of how to respond.

"Of course, Elisha usually has all the leads, so I don't actually believe Val expected to win it."

Carol smiled weakly, still confused by the unending line of chatter.

"And, Elisha, of course, is the only member of the West Egelton Senior High Drama Club that I've never met. She spends all her holidays with her family in California. The all-American spawning ground for oversized blonds."

As if on cue, David White entered the kitchen. He wore a white turtleneck and carried the forest green vest and the Scandinavian sweater. They oozed muddy water.

Carol stared at him with undisguised fury. She realized David had lied to her about the party. He knew Elisha would be away. He had used his girlfriend's absence to trick Carol into thinking he had given up the old relationship.

David ignored Carol. "Mrs. R., I'm sorry to bother you, but Val suggested I'd better have you check these things out." He held up his outerwear.

"No problem, David; hardly a bother. Take some cider, while I rinse these out." She lifted the muddy garments from his arms and left.

David washed his hands at the kitchen sink.

Staring down into her mug, Carol said, "I want to go home."

"And you expect me to take you?"

"You brought me."

"That's great, just great!" he exclaimed, crossing the kitchen to gaze down at Carol. "After all the hassle getting here!"

Carol looked up. David's brilliant green eyes bored into her bright blue ones.

"I should have expected it! Elisha's right about you, Little Miss Muffet."

Carol took a deep breath. She spoke slowly and carefully. "David, you lied to me, tricked me, and embarrassed me; the least you can do is have the courtesy to drive me home!"

"Courtesy! I tried to be courteous to you and wound up in an iced mud bath!"

"Dragging me about like a kid who missed her nap is not courtesy!"

"Well, if you want to go home, you'll just have to walk!" David stomped toward the door. "As far as I'm concerned this date is over!"

Carol watched his broad shoulders and golden waves retreat. She remembered the unsent pass, the smoky theatre, the empty parking lot, the sleazy restaurant, the lies about Elisha, the missed lunch date, more lies about Elisha, the late pick up, the empty gas tank, the humiliation of being handled like a child in front of the whole drama club . . . Len's right, I've been an incredibly slow learner! She concluded, unhappily.

The door opened and half a dozen girls came into the kitchen. They surrounded the cider pot.

Carol sunk into the cushions hoping they would not notice her. Marie, a slender dark girl who played the part of a gossipping student, was the first to speak. "Hey, are you okay?"

Carol nodded because she felt too embarrassed to say anything.

The girl continued. "We were beginning to worry; you looked okay walking toward the steps, but no one's seen you since your glorious entrance."

Surprised by Marie's statement, Carol gathered her courage. "I'm fine, thanks. This is just such a nice room, I . . ."

"That's for sure!" interrupted Lena, the senior in charge of the art crew, "all our best parties always end up in here. Carol's just being clever by starting here!"

"Carol seems to be clever at everything. I don't think anyone else, ever, put David White in his place before," observed a member of the prop committee.

"Right, a mud puddle's just the place for a male chauvinist pig."

All the girls laughed.

"Yeah, did you see that look of pure defeated macho on his face as he went down!"

The laughter took on a wicked edge.

The art crew head added, "I'll bet David listens a lot more carefully from now on!"

As the laughter increased, Carol began to relax. Her feelings of embarrassment and isolation melted with the knowledge that the other girls understood more than she believed they could.

"I always seem to miss the best jokes," commented Len as he pushed open the swinging door.

"Is this where you're all hiding?" asked John from the light crew, following Len into the kitchen.

Len placed his hand on Carol's shoulder. "I thought maybe you got a bit of a mud bath."

"No," Carol smiled, "David was just telling me what a fun date I am."

"That's okay, you can ride home with us, if you don't mind being on the cleanup squad," offered Marie.

"Wait a minute, where's she going to sit?" protested a girl Carol did not remember. "We played sardines all the way out here!"

"She can sit on my lap, but only," Len made a broad bit out of winking, "if she promises not to kick."

"You've forgotten, Val lives here! She won't be going back with us," said Tina, the senior from the art crew.

"That's right, we have an extra seat."

"Nuts, foiled again!" exclaimed Len wrapping an invisible cloak across his face, rolling his eyes, and ending with a sidewise wink at Carol.

She laughed with the others. But at the same time Carol recognized a surprising touch of disappointment. She realized that for a moment she had looked forward to sitting in Len's lap.

chapter
✦✶ 9 ✶✦

"Carol, walk to the edge of the stage," Mr. Carter directed. "Now, turn right and walk; turn left and walk."

Wearing the red plaid skirt with its matching ruffled blouse for the first time, Carol followed her drama teacher's instructions. As she moved around on the stage Carol peered out past the lights into the empty auditorium. This would be the last time she would play Mandy to the unoccupied green seats.

Carol wondered how late the dress rehearsal would run. The clock at the back of the auditorium pointed to ten after four. The last bus would leave in a few minutes. Carol realized that if she was modeling the first of her six costumes, the dress parade alone, without the rehearsal, might take the club until past dinner time.

Nancy Rodgers had explained that this evening was intended more for the technicians and crew than the actors. She suggested that each student tell his or her parents not to expect them home until after eleven. And she had organized car pools to insure that everyone would get home.

Extracurricular had as many characters as Len and Mr. Carter believed the stage could comfortably hold. The idea was to give a chance to be on stage with at least one line to say to every member of the club who wanted one. Occasionally, a student who auditioned poorly blossomed with the help of make-up and applause.

93

"Add more rouge to your cheeks; the lights make you look like a ghost. The costume's fine. Go change and send in anyone who's ready."

A boy playing the part of a student rushed onto the stage before Carol could call him.

A large portion of her wardrobe hung in the costume room—all the frills and bows that Carol had left unworn since she started at West Egelton Senior High School. Her mother had been delighted when Carol explained these would be her costumes for Len's show. Mrs. Clark had even volunteered to deliver the clothing to the school.

Mrs. Cooper, the round and silver-haired image of the ideal grandmother, had instructed her Home Ec. classes to starch every ruffle until the garments practically walked by themselves. She helped Carol remove the stiff blouse and replaced it with another, equally flounced and hardened.

"I'm glad you only do this show once. All this ironing and starching makes me feel like a new bride in the 1940s," she said with the lilt of an Irish accent.

Carol had difficulty finding a correct response for Mrs. Cooper's observations. But Mrs. Cooper never acted as if she expected any. Carol knew that the students adored her.

"Mr. C. says I need more rouge."

"Well, don't you go touching it! In two seconds flat you'll be covered in red, like the body in a post-war mystery film."

She adjusted Carol's second skirt and blouse, a pastel of pink and blue gingham. While tying a rose satin bow in Carol's hair, she shouted in her sing-song voice, "Pat, oh, Patricia, where are you?"

"Coming, Mrs. Cooper." A heavy girl dressed in dark clothing and red, wrist-band pin cushion, rushed into the room.

"Mr. C. says more rouge."

"Sure thing!" she grabbed a plastic jar and dabbed at Carol's cheeks. Meanwhile, Mrs. Cooper arranged the points of a lacy handkerchief to show from the skirt pocket.

Carol thought, I feel like a three-tiered birthday cake! But she said nothing.

All this effort was to make Mandy believable and Carol look good on stage. The difference between herself and her character remained uppermost in Carol's mind. She had been encouraged by Mr. Carter to use this difference to help build her performance.

Surveying her work, Mrs. Cooper remarked, "What a shame no one looks like this anymore."

Pat laughed, "This is a modern dress show!"

"I know, but the girls don't wear these sweet, young clothes anymore. Chic seems to mean stark, such a pity."

Both girls laughed, while Mrs. Cooper circled Carol, checking that everything appeared perfect. "Go show Mr. C."

Carol hurried toward the stage door. The discomfort of her make-up and costume made Carol feel as if she moved like a windup toy. She passed the girls' and boys' dressing rooms. She would have liked to be with the other kids, but her changes would be impossible in the small space allotted to each student actor.

Everyone's costumes were drawn from their everyday clothes. And, Mrs. Cooper observed, the simpler designs of jeans, A-line skirts, and easy care tops required no special dressing assistance. Pat and a few other Home Ec. majors were overseeing the make-up and accessories.

". . . table and my cosmetics and don't you dare to . . ." Elisha's voice carried her quarrel into the dimly lit hallway.

Carol was glad to close the soundproof stage door and

leave Elisha's complaints behind her.

Len and several of the crew were reinforcing a sliding wood brace with a square cast-iron weight. His hands were supporting the framed canvas wall called a flat. He wiggled his eyebrows at Carol as she walked onto the stage.

She turned to wave, grateful for the warm feeling of confidence Len gave her. Whenever rehearsals had fallen apart, he had rushed to her side. He had coached her on the lines and taught her the special language of the theatre: "Heads up means duck and protect your head before something falls on it!" "To move up or down on stage means to move away from or closer to the audience. Telling someone to 'break a leg' means you wish them good luck but don't want to attract the evil eye, that would bring them bad luck."

It all sounded so inside out and backwards, Carol was sure Len had made it up. But everyone else seemed to use these words and phrases exactly the way he had explained them.

"Heads up," called a male voice behind Carol's back.

She whirled, looking toward the ceiling grids. A long row of pipes dangled from ropes that held them at various heights as much as two stories from the stage floor. From where she stood Carol could see the lower edge of the huge American flag that the school always displayed during assemblies, two dark green velvet curtains, and several dozen black, metal, theatrical lighting fixtures connected with what looked like miles of thick wires. But she did not see anything falling.

Still staring at the grid, Carol bumped directly into David. She jumped back, but not soon enough.

"Good enough to eat!" he laughed and reached out to pinch her cheek. He wore dark slacks, a white button-down shirt, and a tweed coat with leather elbow patches.

His face was colored in dark and light areas to add age for his role as the teacher.

"You've spoiled my make-up!" She patted at the damaged area.

"You could say hello before you start complaining."

"You could say hello instead of making me angry!"

"Has anyone ever told you you're cute when you're angry?" He gave her his best smile, dimples and all.

"Yes, you; almost every time we have a rehearsal!" She found herself returning his smile easily, without a lump in her throat or a flutter in her pulse.

"Can't fault a guy for trying!" He held up his hands, and they both laughed.

Most of this conversation had been repeated so often, Carol felt as if it were an additional dialogue that was trying to fight its way onto the stage. She and David related best through the formality of Len's words or a set exchange such as this. The residue of pain and anger from their two failed dates, still remained unresolved. But their daily contact at rehearsals required a truce. This gave them the illusion of talking without the strain of communicating.

"Next! Anyone in the wings?" called Mr. Carter.

"Yes, coming," answered Carol. Stepping around David, she walked out between the teaser curtains that hid the sides of the stage, called wings, from view. She stood still under the hot lights that flooded the half-built classroom set.

"Come to center, turn around; very nice, thank you, Carol."

She started toward the wings thinking she was getting the idea of what he expected. Maybe the costume parade would not take all night.

Mr. Carter stopped her. "Use the door!" he demanded.

Readjusting her direction, Carol walked between the

two tape marks attached to the floor that were supposed to represent an invisible entranceway. By the time all the costumes were reviewed the crew was supposed to have the entire classroom standing in place.

There's always something else, she thought. As she moved through the left wing, Carol saw Len standing alone backstage by the lighting control board.

"Where's the step-and-fetch-it brigade?" she asked, noticing his blue, cotton work shirt looked as starched and ironed as her ruffled blouse.

"Raiding the gym for extra weights."

"For real!" Carol's shock registered in her voice.

"We always get them back before they're missed."

"Standard procedure?"

"Sort of a Robin Hood action; their department's a lot better funded than Mr. C.'s."

"That's to prepare us for the real world!"

"I like your costume. You really do look just like I imagined Mandy would look."

"Well, you created her." Carol curtsied and started for the exit. She felt equally flattered and annoyed by Len's observation. "I have to change."

"Wait," Len hurried to catch her. "You didn't let me finish!"

They walked under the red lit exit sign. "I was going to say, but Mandy's not you. You're much more..." He closed the soundproof stage door. Before he could continue his sentence the hall filled with people.

"Hey, Len, we got 'em!" shouted Kevin, a skinny boy with bright orange hair.

"Shhh!!!" cautioned his two companions.

"Come on!" groaned carrot-topped Kevin.

The three boys pushed a laundry cart that appeared full of towels, but it clunked as they rolled it along.

"No! Stop it! Stop it, now!" Elisha fled from the girls'

dressing room followed by Pat, the costume assistant. "You stick me once more, and you won't have to wear a pin cushion!"

"But, the hem . . ." They dodged the crowd and pushed through the stage door.

Mrs. Cooper popped out of her cubicle. "Carol, why are you loitering about! You look like a chicken waiting to cross the road." She grabbed Carol's hand and pulled her along the corridor. "Come along, now, my dear."

Len shrugged, "Catch you later."

Carol barely permitted Mrs. Cooper to zip up her blue and white dotted swiss. She rushed backstage. But Len was with the crew on the catwalks, twelve feet above her head.

As Carol walked toward the wings, Pat grabbed the end of her rose satin hair ribbon. She yanked it off Carol's head and reached over to fluff the matted curls.

"Thanks!" Carol said softly. Then she carefully stepped through the marks of the invisible doorway.

A loud hiss of anger cut across the empty stage. "I'm tired and I just don't care!"

A harsh female whisper interrupted, "You! you! you! All I hear is you!"

"It's the same thing every time!" answered the quieter male tones. Suddenly the murmur jumped to a shout, "Elisha, don't!"

"Quiet backstage!" yelled Mr. Carter from the front of the auditorium. "Okay, Carol walk down center and . . ."

"Heads up! Heads up!" exclaimed a chorus of hysterical male voices.

"Carol move!" ordered Len from the catwalk.

She leaped downstage toward the audience and heard his voice continue to give orders.

"David, grab the . . ."

An iron pipe crashed down from the grid. Its right

99

end banged against the standing portion of the set.

Carol heard the flat collapse. The wood cracked and the canvas tore. But she stared, mesmerized, at the left end of the heavy metal bar as it bounced to the stage floor leaving dents in the polished wood.

"Anyone hurt?" called the male voice that Carol recognized at full volume to be David's.

Mr. Carter raced up the aisle, while Len tore down the ladder. They arrived where Carol stood on the apron, almost simultaneously.

"You're fine! It never came close to you!" Mr. Carter shouted as if to terrify her out of her fright.

Carol felt her hands start to shake. The tremor moved up her arms and into her shoulders. Her knees collapsed as Len slipped his arm around her waist.

"Take care of her, Len!" directed Mr. Carter as he dashed across the stage. "Who released that pipe?"

Len helped Carol to sit on the edge of the apron. Their legs swung into the orchestra pit. He kept his arm around her.

"Mr. C's right, you know; it really didn't come anywhere near you," he murmured in a soothing tone.

Carol leaned against Len's side. She barely felt his arms around her waist; it did not help her to stop shaking. From the stage behind her came the sounds of the crew assessing and repairing the damage. Carol could not bring herself to turn around. She stared at the empty green seats.

After a few moments she replied to Len's statement, "I know; it's just..." Carol's voice trailed off as the shaking began to increase.

"If you want to cry, I'm all equipped." Len pushed a blue handkerchief into her closed fist. It was as starched as his matching work shirt.

From somewhere backstage came the muttering of angry voices. Elisha's rose, clearly, above the others. "The handle was marked empty!" "But she wasn't hurt!" and, "My father will pay for the repairs!" The words drifted to where Len and Carol sat; their unpleasant, imperious tone rang out from the otherwise, unintelligible argument.

Carol squeezed Len's handkerchief. The stiffened square of cotton irritated her hand. It reminded Carol of her continuing puzzlement at the discrepancies in Len's wardrobe. Her curiosity overcame her fear.

"Who starched your clothing?"

Startled by her unexpected question, he responded earnestly, "I did. Did I do it wrong?"

She started to laugh and noticed that the shaking had stopped. "No, you did it fine. Only you seem to have done everything you own."

"Dad and I have been trying to make the house and everything perfect. We may have gone too far." He grinned and squeezed her with his left arm, which was still around her waist. "That's what I wanted to tell you about out in the hall before."

Carol tightened up and started to shake again.

Len stopped speaking to reach for Carol's quivering hands.

"I just keep thinking that was up there all the time." She looked at Len, her large blue eyes brimming with tears. "It could have come down at any moment."

"No!" He rocked her gently backward and forward. "No, its got locks and safeties and handles. Pipes can't possibly come down without a human being to release them."

"It was just so sudden!" she protested.

"I know it felt that way to you, but it really moved

very slowly. There are counter weights on every pipe. Come on," he jumped to the auditorium floor, "I'll show you."

She allowed him to assist her to a standing position and guide her up the auditorium stairs. At the top of the steps Carol froze.

"I can't go on the stage!"

"You've been on it every day for two months!"

"I can't." Her whole body vibrated with terror.

"All right, we won't walk on the stage. We'll just step on the apron and slip behind the arch." He wrapped his left arm around Carol's shoulders and held both her hands in his right one. He drew her around the performing area of the stage to the counterbalance system.

Carol stared at the extended metal counter that stretched along the entire wall. She knew she had passed it every afternoon when she attended rehearsal, but she had never noticed it. The profusion of handles, ropes, and weights made her think of the exotic exercise machines she saw advertised in her mother's favorite magazines.

Len chose an empty pipe near the apron. He warned the crew, who were just completing the repair job, and showed Carol how to operate the safety, release, and ropes.

She quickly accepted his evaluation of the safety of the counterbalance system. No pipe could come flying from the grid without human assistance.

"I guess it was the noise and damage that frightened me!"

"I'm glad you realized it—for a moment there, I thought I'd have to play Mandy," he teased her.

"I'd love to see you in this dress." Carol flipped her hands over the starched ruffles. Their stiffness reminded her Len had not finished explaining what it was he had started to say. "What were you trying to tell me before..." she paused, "all the excitement."

Len hesitated, "Well, it's about my Mom; she's been sick in the hospital for the last few months."

"You've never said anything." It was Carol's turn to reach for Len's hands. She held them with the same gentle pressure he had given her.

"Some of the kids know. There's nothing anyone can do. Anyway, what I wanted to tell you is that she'll be here to see the show!"

"Then I guess I'll have to do it!" Carol smiled up at Len.

The crew had finished working on the broken flat. Carol and Len were alone in the auditorium. They slowly walked across the stage together, tightly holding hands.

"Except for the marks on the floor, it might never have happened," she said with amazement when they reached the light board on the opposite side of the stage. Len leaned over and brushed her forehead with his lips.

Carol felt the warmth linger moments after his gentle touch departed. Her forehead seemed to glow. She tilted her face up at Len's. He turned toward her. Carol realized that he stood only a few inches taller than she. A warm rush flowed across her face and traveled down through her body as she felt Len place his hands on her shoulders. She drew a deep breath.

The stage door crashed open with an enormous bang. The noise froze Carol like an animal caught at night in the glare of a car's headlights.

"Where's she?"

"Are you all right?"

"What idiot...?"

Questions flew as the cast and crew members surrounded Carol and Len.

Len gave her a shake and patted vigorously at her upper arms as if he were trying to wake her from a trance.

Carol released her breath. She stepped back at the same moment that Len let go of her shoulders. The chaotic concern of the other club members did nothing to offset either her disappointment or confusion.

David's voice cut through the noise, "Carol's okay! See, the author's busy giving her his new line!"

Len broke into a burst of relieved laughter, "I was just checking to protect my interest in the show." He winked and leered, slipping into his imitation of a silent movie villain.

"Is it *The Perils of Pauline* we're playin', then?" inquired Mrs. Cooper. Her accent deepened with her concern as she maneuvered her way to Carol's side.

Looking at the kindly Home Ec. teacher, Carol just stopped herself from blurting out, but Len should be the hero not the villain! She blushed and smiled, imagining the whoops and guffaws that phrase would have released.

"I'm glad to see you're all right, I was afraid we'd have to alter your costumes to cover the dents."

Everyone, except Carol, responded with wild laughter. She stood in the center of the crowd and felt lonely.

Am I all right, she wondered. For a moment I thought Len was going to kiss me. I guess—Carol glanced at her friend as he clowned with the other students—I just wanted him to kiss me. I know he likes me as a friend and an actress, but...

"A bad dress rehearsal means a good show." Frank Martin, the boy who played Chris, pounded Carol's back while quoting the old theatrical proverb.

"If you all keep standing around here, there won't be any kind of a dress," observed Mr. Carter. He nodded to Nancy Rodgers.

"First act places in fifteen minutes! Everyone but the crew clear the stage!" She shouted, asserting her authority as the stage manager.

chapter
⋆⋆ 10 ⋆⋆

Carol hid her blushes in a huge bouquet of roses, while the audience stamped on the floor, clapped, and whistled. The whole cast, as well as Len and Mr. Carter, had taken two full sets of bows. The curtain closed, and what felt to Carol like dozens of hands pushed her out between the folds for this final tribute. David rushed out from the wings to present her with the flowers.

It's all too much, she thought. I can't believe the play's over! And they liked it! Len must be pleased. I wish he were here instead of David. Actually, she thought, he should be here instead of either of us. My knees are knocking almost as loud as they're clapping, she realized.

Before the show everyone had whispered and tried to keep Carol calm. They wished her "broken legs" and assorted other disasters. But Carol had felt perfectly calm.

"Cool and collected like the iceman in winter," observed Mrs. Cooper while she checked Carol's costume for the third time.

Even when the show started, Carol walked through the door that had replaced the tape marks into the make-believe classroom with perfect confidence. Mandy's words and movements kept her so busy that she forgot to be nervous. However, now that the show was over, Carol felt the sweeping movements of an enormous company of the traditional butterflies tickling her innards.

She removed her nose from the bouquet and whispered

into the thunderous applause, "Thank you, David. These roses are incredible."

"You did an incredible job; you deserve incredible flowers."

"Oh, David," Carol smiled at the handsome senior and curtsied again.

He bowed and kissed her hand while muttering, "We'd better go in before they get blisters." He grasped the curtain. In a gesture of dramatic gallantry, he held it open while Carol stepped through the drapery into the additional applause of the cast and crew.

"Thank you, that's enough." Carol shook her head, no, and laughed. "It's too much; more than too much!" She knew only the people standing nearest her could hear her embarrassed attempts to discourage their enthusiasm. But she did not want to shout her discomfort loud enough for the audience to hear on the other side of the curtain.

The glaring stage lights had been changed for caged work bulbs, but the heat remained. There were too many people in the narrow space walled off by the make-believe classroom.

Carol felt her frills droop and her make-up melt. She wished she could rush into the costume room and fling off the stiff, ruffled, little-girl clothes. Playing Mandy required displaying all the qualities Carol disliked. Now that the play was over, she could see that the role had helped her understand herself, but she wanted to be done with it.

People continued to enter the acting space. Teachers, friends, and family of the cast and crew pressed against the canvas flats and the velvet curtain like molecules of air filling a balloon. The applause finally stopped. Small groups formed as the outsiders located those they had come on stage to find.

Before Carol could take advantage of the change, she

was surrounded by the girls from her English class.

"I just loved it when you kissed him!" squealed Peggy.

"Bill almost started to cry," sighed Lenore.

"Your eyes were a bit shiny, too," noted Maris.

"If you hadn't been so involved with your spitball . . ."

Carol did not reply. They continued arguing around her, but the girls did not seem to notice her lack of response. She was busy looking for Len. When their eyes met, Carol felt the noise, heat, and fear melting away. She saw him call her name, but could not lip-read the rest of his message.

Don't be foolish, Carol warned herself, he's congratulating or thanking you; that's all. She answered herself impatiently, well, what else do you expect from him. For a moment she recalled the touch of his hands on her shoulders, and the look on his face just before the stage door had crashed open. That was your imagination—remember!

These thoughts flashed through her mind while she strained her eyes to understand his lips. Suddenly Carol found she was staring at a brown wool suit and a maroon tie.

"Oh, Mr. Brockton!" Carol stepped back, startled to see her homeroom teacher. The curtain behind her prevented her from edging off the stage.

"An excellent performance, Miss Clark."

"Thank you."

"The play was very good, too. But you created Mandy as if she were written for you. How did you feel playing someone so different from yourself?"

"At first, I was afraid of her," Carol paused, surprised to find herself speaking calmly with the man she secretly called the morning terror. "But Len, Len Whitkins, the author, helped me." She was pleased that someone recognized the difference between herself and her character, particularly someone she did not know well.

"Oh, darling, you looked absolutely adorable," interrupted her mother, elbowing her way through the crowd. "I don't know why you can't dress that way all the time! It's so attractive on you."

"Mr. Brockton, this is my mother, Mrs. Clark," Carol introduced them. She felt her blush returning. "Mother, Mr. Brockton's my homeroom teacher," Carol said, trying to hold off the inevitable flood of clothing commentary.

"Oh, Mr. Brockton, I'm so pleased to meet you. Now, you see Carol every day, don't you? Wouldn't you agree that she looked lovely tonight on the stage?"

Carol wished there was a trapdoor under her feet. She would have liked to vanish in a puff of smoke, or any other way at all. She could not imagine facing Mr. Brockton on Monday morning.

But her homeroom teacher smiled benignly at Mrs. Clark before he replied, "Of course Carol looked lovely on stage tonight. She's a fine actress, and the costumes helped delineate her character."

Mrs. Clark started to press her question, but Mr. Brockton turned his body to exclude her from his conversation with her daughter.

"I only wished to congratulate you; I won't detain you any longer." He took Carol's hand and shook it with great solemnity.

She smiled at him politely and was astonished to see her dignified teacher wink. The butterflies escaped in a string of uncontrollable giggles as he slipped away through the crowd.

"Don," called her mother, "Don, where are you?" She turned to Carol, "Your father was right behind me. I can't imagine where he's got to now!"

Carol searched the crowd until she found her father beaming like a lighthouse in the ocean of her admirers.

Still giggling, she waved and took a deep breath to call him. Instead of a shout, the giggles turned into hiccups.

"Hold your breath," commanded her mother, twisting around to see at whom her daughter had been waving.

"I (hic) can't (hic) breathe, (hic)" Carol giggled.

Mrs. Clark took her daughter's hand, and they started working their way back toward the stage door. However, every few feet people would embrace and praise Carol. And she hiccuped her gratitude into their faces.

"Bend over and exhale."

"It's all (hic) right (hic)."

"Get a paper bag! Does anyone have a paper bag?"

"I'll (hic) be fine (hic)."

"Water! There's water in the dressing rooms. Someone bring some water!"

"(Hic) Don't (hic) bother (hic) I'm (hic) coming (hic)."

Their progress through the crowd resembled that of a small child pulling a cart with a broken wheel.

Carol felt someone lift the roses and take her freed arm.

"Len!" His unexpected presence startled away Carol's hiccups. At the same time the crowd seemed to thin. The three moved easily toward the red exit. "I couldn't understand what you were trying to say."

"I know." He helped Mrs. Clark guide Carol into the hall, which appeared to be just as crowded as the stage had been.

"Aren't the roses beautiful," Carol said as Len returned them, "David bought them for me."

"David! The Club bought them! Did he say he did?"

"Not exactly. Do you mean he tricked me again?"

"I know, some people are slow learners!"

Students, friends, and parents pressed in among the club members as if they were a New York road company that would be gone at midnight. Carol and her mother

110

found themselves pushed against the wall near the stage entrance.

The door of the girls' dressing room flew open. Elisha and an older woman, who was in every other respect an exact replica of her, stepped into the hallway. They both wore floor-length red capes. Like magic, a path cleared itself. The two started their dramatic sweep along the corridor toward the exits. The older woman stopped in front of Carol and Mrs. Clark.

"A most interesting interpretation," she pronounced. Without moving her head she lowered her eyes to look down at Carol.

Before Carol could respond they were gone, and the masses had moved in to fill the hall.

Mr. Clark appeared at Carol's side. He kissed her cheek without a word. She gave him one of her roses. He inhaled its fragrance and handed the flower to his wife. She smiled and kissed her husband's cheek.

Mrs. Clark cradled the flower while she spoke to her daughter. "David's such a gentleman; we haven't seen him in the last few weeks. Such a good-looking boy and . . ."

Knowing no way to discourage her, Carol simply decided to ignore her mother. She turned to speak with Len, but she found that he had vanished. Instead of Len, Mrs. R. and Val stood next to her. They were trying to edge along the wall to the exit.

"I seem to have just missed meeting Elisha," said Val's mother, smiling at Carol with understanding.

"Carol, you were wonderful! I'm glad you won the part of Mandy."

"Thanks, Val." Carol handed both redheads roses.

"A bunch of us are going to the Soda Shack. Do you want to come along?"

"Sure! First, I have to change out of this get-up; if I

can only get to the costume room."

"The place will clear out in a few minutes," promised Mrs. R.

"You're sure?" asked Mr. Clark with disbelief.

"Watch and see, I've been attending these shows for eight years." She slipped along the wall behind the Clarks while they talked.

"Then you must be an expert," he teased.

Carol remembered her manners as the mother and daughter moved away down the hall. "Mrs. R. and Val, these are my parents, Mr. and Mrs. Clark," she called at their slowly retreating backs.

"Nice to meet you; look forward to seeing you at the Soda Shack," returned Mrs. R. "We'll save you a place."

Exactly as Mrs. R. predicted, the hall and dressing rooms began to empty. Carol and her parents reached the costume room without any additional problems or delay.

"Well, my girl, I hear it went like a hot knife through butter!" Carol handed her a rose. And this time her manners were thoroughly correct. "Mrs. Cooper, I'd like you to meet my mother and father, Mr. and Mrs. Clark."

"A lovely girl you have raised," said Mrs. Cooper, waving the flower for emphasis.

"Well, you've done more to make her look lovely tonight than I've been able to accomplish all year!" exclaimed Mrs. Clark with exasperation.

Carol began to feel overwhelmed by the inevitable discussion concerning her taste in clothing.

"Lovely is as lovely does."

"Excuse me, Mrs. Cooper," Carol interrupted. "Mom, Dad, I have to speak to someone; please stay here, I'll be back in a few minutes." She clasped the bouquet in her arms and fled. She knew her mother would continue talking in her absence.

There was no one Carol had to speak to, but she found herself searching the dressing room, the backstage area, the catwalks, the wings, and the set. Whenever she encountered members of the cast or crew, Carol offered them roses. The girls accepted, but most of the boys laughingly refused. If they had all accepted, there would not have been enough flowers for everyone. Even so, by the time Carol stepped between the curtains onto the apron of the stage, she held only two roses and some green tissue paper.

The auditorium was almost empty. The last stragglers waited by the doors. Several loud claps brought Carol's attention to a couple seated on the aisle. Actually, the dark, curly-headed man sat in the aisle seat; the slender, fair woman wearing a gold and black hostess gown sat in a wheelchair.

"Carol Clark, the leading lady of West Egelton Senior High, I presume."

Suddenly Carol realized she had been searching for someone, "Yes, have you seen the author, Leonard Whitkins?" she asked from the stage.

"If you'll do us the honor of sitting here for a few minutes, we'll do our very best to produce him," replied the man with an assumed British accent.

Without any further introduction, Carol recognized that this couple must be Len's parents. She walked down the stage steps and held out the remaining roses.

"Mrs. Whitkins, these are for you."

"Oh, no," said Len's mother in a soft whisper-like voice. "Those are yours. Len told us how hard you worked. You certainly deserve them."

"He spoke about me?" Carol felt a tingle of surprised pleasure.

"Len told us all about the show while it was in production."

113

"Oh, yes, of course," Carol paused before remembering her intentions. "If you had not had Len, I would not have had anything to work at! You must take the flowers." She lay them on Mrs. Whitkins' knees.

All three laughed. Mrs. Whitkins' murmur of gratitude was drowned by Len's entrance.

"Ah, ha!" He popped his head through the center of the curtains. "Leave them alone for one minute and they start to plot." He paced the apron.

"Aye, Capt'n, we 'ave caught a stowaway!" answered his father in Cockney.

"A stowaway, humm..." Len swung himself off the apron and landed on the auditorium floor with a thud. "To the plank with her, me hearties!"

"How about to the Soda Shack?" suggested his mother.

"Let me treat you both to their hamburger special," Mr. Whitkins held out some money to his son.

"That may be worse than walking the plank," Len agreed, joining Carol and his family. He kissed his mother and asked, "Won't you be coming with us?"

"No, darling, I'm much too tired."

"Are you sure?" Carol asked with obvious disappointment.

"Yes, dear, this is my first night home from the hospital. Your performance has made it very special, but I'm exhausted."

"Thank you," replied Carol, flushing slightly. This soft spoken compliment meant more to her than all the applause, the roses, or the other praise she had received.

"No, thank you," smiled Mr. Whitkins.

"I asked Len to invite you to join us for brunch on Sunday, but I gather my son has neglected to deliver the invitation."

"Ah, Mom, come on, I haven't had a chance."

Carol was surprised to realize that this charming woman

could have exactly the same effect on Len that her own mother had on her.

"Thank you, if it's all right with Len, I'd be delighted." Carol's heart sped up. She felt the beat of her pulse race against her fingertips. And the place where Len had touched her forehead felt glowing hot.

Everyone's attention turned to Len. "Of course, it's all right," he half shouted. Then in tones of frustration, he added, "That's what I was trying to tell you backstage!"

Carol heard more in the tone than the words. She was disappointed. It's still just a friendship to him. Why do parents do these things to their kids?

"Oh, my goodness! I forgot, my parents are still in the costume room!" Carol started up the aisle; she turned and walked backwards while she spoke. "It was a pleasure to meet you, and I look forward to seeing you on Sunday." Carol paused at the bottom of the stairs to the stage. "Where and at what time?" she asked somewhat breathlessly.

"You can come anytime after ten-thirty," replied Mrs. Whitkins. "Len can give you the address."

"Nonsense," boomed her husband, "we'll send the chauffeur around at ten!" "James," Mr. Whitkins addressed his son, "After you drop us at the castle, the car's yours for the evening."

"Dad, I won't go out if you two aren't coming."

"Don't be ridiculous. This is your party for your first play!" insisted Len's father. "Besides, it's my first chance to be alone with my beautiful wife."

"Oh, Robert," sighed Mrs. Whitkins.

Feeling awkward and half-forgotten, Carol paused before stepping through the curtains. "Goodbye, I'll see you on Sunday." She hoped it sounded more cheerful than she felt. It would not be any kind of party without

Len. But then, she reminded herself, he does not feel that way about you!

"Goodbye, dear."

"We'll be looking forward to it!"

Both the stage and the hallway were totally deserted. Carol found it almost eerie that the crowds of people seemed to have vanished in such a short period of time.

"I suppose you're right, girls aren't wearing these pretty things anymore," sighed Mrs. Clark as Carol drew near the costume room. "I'll just have to get used to letting her find her own style."

Carol entered the room with the feeling that a very powerful magician must have waved both arms hard to bring about that change. She could barely believe her ears.

"Mrs. Cooper has been discussing the new female fashions," Mr. Clark explained to his startled daughter.

"Mrs. Cooper, thank you!" Carol said with delight, then thinking of her mother, "I'm sorry I left you waiting so long."

"That's all right, my dear, it's been my pleasure gettin' to know your charmin' family." She handed Carol her jeans and turtleneck. "You'd best be wearing some of these new female fashions."

"Thanks! This time I promise I really will be right back."

"I've heard that somewhere before!" teased her father.

"Take your time, we'll pack up the costumes while you change," called Mrs. Clark as her daughter raced down the hall to the girls' dressing room.

Carol pulled off her blouse as she crossed the empty room to the sink. She wiped away the messy cosmetic stains and bits of damp tissue before washing her face. The soap and water removed everything but her eye make-up. In order to save time, she left that alone. Carol

116

stepped out of the now damp and creased skirt, and slipped on the pants and sweater.

Looking down at the crumpled remains of the little girl, Mandy, Carol wondered if she could just leave the clothing there with the used tissues and the empty cosmetics containers. But she knew her mother's new resolve would not stretch to the careless loss of a good skirt and blouse, even if they were ones her daughter planned never to wear again.

Grabbing the unwanted garments, Carol hurried back to the costume room, where she relinquished them to Mrs. Cooper.

"You look beautiful; well worth waiting for," said her father, placing a kiss on her uncombed head.

"I'll have this dry and packed before you can whistle "Danny Boy!" Mrs. Cooper handed Carol a small shopping bag and took the worn clothing to the ironing board. "You'd best be puttin' away your trinkets."

"You don't have to iron that dress!" Carol protested.

"I've got the board out, and I think it would be a nice gesture."

"What are these, dear?" asked Mrs. Cooper drawing her daughter's attention away from the busy Home Ec. teacher.

"Those were presents from the other kids." Carol picked up a red, satin, stilleto-healed shoe filled with jellybeans. "Have some," she offered the candy to her parents and Mrs. Cooper before placing it on the bottom of the bag. She knew David had received the mate.

"There seem to be an awful lot of shoes," commented her father while Carol pinned a pair of ceramic 1930s style pumps to her turtleneck.

"They're for good luck, like at a wedding," said Mrs. Clark with absolute assurance.

Carol chose not to offer any additional information.

She packed a small stuffed pillow in the shape of a high heel and a glass perfume bottle with the same shape. It was marked, "Midnight Magic."

Frank, the boy who played Chris, had given it to her with a warning not to open it. He said that it smelled like essence of rotted pumpkin. Carol had foolishly ignored his advice. One sniff convinced her it had been blended to drive the white mice wild.

Just as Carol completed her packing, Mrs. Cooper handed Mr. Clark a large cardboard carton. "Well, that's the lot; if you're ready, I'll be goin' over to the Soda Shack." She smiled at Carol, who hurried to pull on her winter coat and collect her shopping bag. "I want to buy a round for my hardworkin' girls."

"Thank you for your help. I'd never have been able to get through the show without you."

"It was my pleasure," she said as they entered the hall.

"And thank you for the advice," said Mrs. Clark.

"Well, for that I think I'll be well repaid," Mrs. Cooper winked at Carol's parents and turned to check the lock on the costume room door. "You go on, I have to lock up."

"We'll wait for you in the parking lot," said Carol's father.

"That's all right, I have my own car."

"This will be our pleasure!" he used her own inflection.

"Well, it might be nice to ride into town with some company," she smiled while switching off the lights and locking the dressing room doors.

The snow-edged parking lot held only a few scattered vehicles. When the four of them reached the car, there was a considerable amount of shifting about, until Carol found herself sitting in the front seat with the costume box.

However, until her father stopped the car in front of the Goodwill collection bin, Carol had no idea of what had been plotted in her absence.

"Well, my dear, we thought you might feel like making a donation to charity," teased the beaming Mrs. Cooper.

"Everything?" Carol asked her mother with astonishment.

"Whatever you want," replied Mrs. Clark, smiling, "No point keeping them just to attract moths."

Carol recognized a hint of an Irish brogue in her mother's words. "I'd like to keep the red plaid skirt."

"Is that all?" asked Mrs. Clark a bit wistfully.

"Yes," replied her daughter with an assurance that astonished her more than it did her parents or teacher.

"Well, go do it!" ordered Mr. Clark.

"Oh, yes!" Carol opened the cardboard box and carefully removed her skirt. "Everything looks so neat," she addressed the compliment to Mrs. Cooper.

"You can still change your mind," suggested her mother.

"I didn't mean that!" exclaimed Carol. She leaped from the car as if the box were weightless. She raced across the icy sidewalk. Shoving the clothing carton into the dark blue metal slot, Carol shouted, "Goodbye, Mandy!"

Her words formed frosted clouds that hung in the air above the collection box, while she hurried back to the warm car.

"Did you see a canary around here?" asked Mrs. Cooper as Carol slipped into the front seat.

It's too cold for tropical birds," replied Mrs. Clark.

Carol rubbed her cold fingers and continued to grin.

chapter

⋆⋆ 11 ⋆⋆

"The street's packed!" observed Mr. Clark. He inched the car through the traffic blocking Egelton's main shopping area.

"It's always this way after a show," said Mrs. Cooper, studying the crowds on the snow-covered sidewalks.

Passing Bee's Stationery and the ice-cream franchise a block from the Soda Shack, Mr. Clark suggested, "If I drop all of you off in front of the hamburger place, then I'll be able to look for parking alone, and you won't have to wander around in the cold."

"It would be easier to leave the car at home and walk back," quipped his daughter.

"Why don't we do that; I'll walk with you." Mrs. Clark urged her husband. "We could use the exercise."

"Everyone get ready." Mr. Clark slowed the rolling speed of the car to a stop. "Quick, everyone out!"

Mrs. Cooper, Carol, and her mother each flung open a door and climbed into the street.

"Hold it!" Mrs. Clark dashed around the rear of the car to take Carol's place in the front seat.

"Hi, Carol!" called Maris from the sidewalk.

"Carol, you're late," shouted Kevin, taking Maris' hand. They entered the Soda Shack together, releasing the sounds of rock music and shouting through the open door.

"We'll see you in a few minutes." Mr. Clark yelled

to his daughter over the protests of blaring horns and the greetings of her friends.

"Come along, my dear, the girls are sure to have a table."

Staring at the front of the restaurant, Carol hesitated. "You go on. I'll be there in a minute." She noticed that the windows were hung with garlands of plastic mistletoe and sprayed with soapy imitation snowflakes. The make-believe Christmas decorations reminded Carol of a stage set and made her wish for Len's company.

"Are you feelin' all right?" Mrs. Cooper stepped out of the path of five students attempting to harmonize "Jingle Bells" while they walked.

"Sure, I'm fine!" Carol paused to remember standing on this same spot and hoping her date with David White would end up here. She shrugged off the bitter memory of *Citizen Kane* and the Corner Bar. Was that two months ago? The time had flown, vanished, disappeared.

She realized Mrs. Cooper was still waiting. Carol improvised, "I just want to take a minute to look at the sky."

"To see what stars look like?" teased Len, ambling toward Carol and Mrs. Cooper. "Don't you think a mirror would do a better job!"

"Oh, Len!" Carol exclaimed with obvious pleasure.

"Well, well, I see you're in good company! I'll leave you in his care." Mrs. Cooper hurried toward the door. "Don't let her stay out here too long. She'll turn into an icicle."

"I didn't think you were coming!" Carol fought to relax her face muscles, which seemed determined to form a silly grin.

"You heard Dad insist. Besides, I wanted to see you!"

"You did?" Hearing the squeak in her voice betray her emotions, Carol wanted to kick herself.

121

"Yes, I . . ."

"Carol, you looked great on stage!"

"Where are your parents?"

With the perfect timing of vultures, the Havor girls had materialized on the sidewalk beside Len and Carol.

"Were you at the show?" Carol asked with bewildered frustration. She resented their interruption of her conversation with Len.

"Oh, yes, we were all there."

"Mom and Dad thought you looked great, too."

"Clara and Paula Havor, this is Leonard Whitkins. He wrote *Extracurricular*." Carol was careful not to indicate her ignorance of which twin belonged to which name.

"Nice to meet you," Len shook hands with each of the attractively dressed girls.

Their obviously well-padded bodies were covered in identically cut winter jackets, one of blue, and the other of green plaid. Each girl wore wool slacks of a solid color that matched her jacket, and medium-heeled, brown leather boots with a matching bag.

"I thought Carol made it up as she went along."

"Yes, what's her name, you know, the girl, Mary . . ."

"Mandy," corrected Len.

"Oh, yes, Mandy had all Carol's best qualities."

"And she looked so cute!"

"Thank you," Carol tried to deter this flood of half insulting ignorance, "Paula and Clara used to live next door to me and my family."

"Where are your parents?"

"They are coming, aren't they?"

"Sure, my mother will be delighted to see you, too. She mentions you both regularly."

"She does?"

"Oh, good, then she won't mind driving us home."

"Yes, Mom and Dad couldn't find parking, but they knew your folks would be here..."

Carol interrupted, "They won't have the car! We couldn't find parking, either. They're walking."

"We'll have to find a ride!"

"See you next month at your birthday dinner—the fifteenth, right?"

"Yes, I'll see you then," Carol sighed.

The Havor girls hurried through the glass and aluminum door. Neither twin spoke to Len or noticed Carol's relief at their departure.

"What charming company you keep. Do you see them every year on your birthday?"

"Oh, yes, they don't mean any harm." Carol giggled and said, "I sound just like my mother!"

"You sound pretty nice to me."

Carol paused, startled by the unexpected compliment. She smiled weakly and waited for Len to go into one of his acts. She was surprised when he just stood smiling back at her.

"You two planning to compete in an ice sculpture contest?" Elisha's superior tone cut into the moment like a torch. She and David, standing arm in arm, stared through their frosted breath at the other couple.

"Hi Elisha, David," Len stopped looking at Carol to greet them. "I haven't had a chance to tell you what great performances you two gave."

"Well, that's understandable," David grinned. "We've all been so impressed with Carol, it's hard to talk about anyone else."

"That's silly!" Carol protested, blushing furiously enough to be seen even by the light of the street lamps. "Everyone worked hard; I mean, if the whole cast and crew didn't do a good job, nothing I did would have mattered. That sounds dumb, but it's true," she added defensively.

"Sure thing, Goody Two Shoes," teased David.

"It did go surprisingly well, considering..."

David cut into Elisha's comments, "It went great! And we should be thanking Len for a chance to do something more interesting than *Grease*."

"We never seriously considered doing that!" Elisha snapped.

"You vetoed it, because you can't sing! But I was all ready! See!" David pulled a black, plastic comb from his back pocket.

"I don't know about you, but I'm freezing!" Elisha made a swift turn. Her red cape and her white hair flared as she started for the entrance.

Giving Len and Carol a quick shrug, David ran to hold the door for Elisha.

The greasy smell of french fries and hamburgers drifted across the icy sidewalk.

Len raised his eyebrows and asked with near angelic innocence, "Do you sing?"

Carol laughed until she felt tears freezing at the edges of her eyes. "You know, they really do make a match. They're two of a kind, and they deserve each other!"

"What about us?" Len's deep dark eyes looked into Carol's bright blue ones. "Are we two of a kind?"

She inhaled the icy air caught in her throat. This time Carol knew there was no joke intended and no clown act coming. She wanted to say how special and wonderful she thought Len was. Carol forced her mouth to move, but the words refused to form.

Len stepped close to her and tried to use his lips to still the useless motion of hers.

For an awkward moment their action was more like a wrestling match than a kiss. Startled by Len's sudden movement, Carol had jumped back, still mouthing the silent words she could not speak. Her arms flailed for balance. Len reached to steady her, but she miscalculated the distance and unintentionally jerked away, slipping on the icy sidewalk. Before she could fall, he caught her shoulders and gently supported her while their lips met.

Carol wondered briefly if it was the near fall or the romance that made her breath come out in gasps as they experimented with holding each other for the first time.

"You two need a lot more practice!" observed a girl's voice cracking with laughter. "Good thing you're in theatre and not the movies!"

Remembering they were still standing on Center Hill Road, right in the middle of town, Carol pulled away from Len.

"West High finally taught you something useful!"

It took a moment before Carol realized that Mary-Lu stood grinning at her from the shadows. "Is that you? I almost didn't recognize you! Your hair looks like you stuck a finger in a live electric socket!" Carol slapped her hand over her mouth. "Oh, I'm sorry! I didn't mean to be insulting. You just took me by surprise, I..."

"It's okay. Calm down, I won't tell that I caught you in the act!" Mary-Lu laughed. "You're right, this perm isn't one of my better styles."

"Paula and Clara came by before, and I couldn't tell who was which."

"They both seemed like horrors to me!" punned Len.

"I know," said Mary-Lu, "I saw them here and decided to take a walk around the block."

"Len, I want you to meet Mary-Lu, my best friend from junior high."

"You wrote *Extracurricular,* didn't you?"

"Yes, you must have been at the show tonight."

"Sure, I wouldn't miss seeing Carol as a star!" Mary-

Lu and Len grinned at each other over Carol's head. "It was a great play, too."

"If you two are through looking like Cheshire cats, I'd like to go inside. My fingers don't have much flexibility left."

Len grabbed Carol's hands and started to rub them. "Where are your gloves? You shouldn't have stayed out here without them!"

"I accidentally donated them to charity." She noticed their puzzled faces, "I'll explain inside. After all, we don't have to stay out here, you know!"

"I'm sorry," said Len, guiding Carol toward the Soda Shack. "I've been selfish; I kept you out here because I needed a little time to be with you alone."

Carol felt her pulse dance. She considered all the things she wanted to share with Len. Time to be alone together would be wonderful.

"Downtown Egelton is your idea of a place to be alone?" teased Mary-Lu. "Len, my friend, you and I are going to have to have a little talk."

"Well, come inside and we will," Len held open the door.

"No, not now, some other time," Mary-Lu backed away from the noise and the heat. Her bravado melted like the new snowflakes falling on the Soda Shack windows. "I have friends waiting for me at the Corner."

"Come in for a few minutes." urged Carol. In spite of her hopes for some time alone with Len, Carol knew the Soda Shack offered no opportunity for privacy.

"If they've waited this long, a little longer shouldn't hurt," suggested Len.

"No, I just wanted to tell Carol I thought she did a real good job."

"Hey, close that door!" shouted someone inside.

Mary-Lu fled in the direction of the movie theatre.

Her black leather jacket quickly vanished into the shadows.

Carol marveled at the swarming mass contained within the pale wood walls. The room was decorated with dozens of those green plastic garlands and gilt "Merry Christmas" signs. The throng consisted mostly of students. Carol was surprised to realize how many of them were her friends.

"I'm sorry she didn't come with us; I liked her," commented Len as he pulled the door tight against a gust of wind.

"She may have been afraid to meet the other kids; she had a bad experience with David."

"Then she's passed the initiation and should be made a member of the Drama Club."

Before Carol could explain that Mary-Lu's experience differed from her own, the crowd that Len feared closed in around them.

"You two been out there all this time!" yelled someone over the rock music from the jukebox.

"Great show! Do the two of you have anything planned for spring?" asked Dr. Edwards' student teaching assistant, "I'd love to work on it with you."

"Carol, there was a phone call for you," said Frank Martin, getting up from the table nearest the door.

"Sure, a big New York producer, I suppose," she grinned.

"No, for real!" Frank insisted. "Ask Lenore," he said, taking her hand as she stood up. "Or any of them." He gestured at Kevin, Maris, Bill, and Peggy with whom they had been sharing the table.

The other kids gayly nodded agreement over their sodas, burgers, and fries.

"What did they say?" Carol asked, still expecting a joke of some sort.

"I didn't take the message; you'll have to ask around to find out who did." Frank led Lenore out among the dancers.

"Who'd call me here?" Carol looked at Len. She let him guide her through the dangers of the gyrating bodies on the dance floor.

Nancy Rodgers looked over the shoulder of her dark-haired partner. "Carol, did you hear there was a telephone call for you?"

"Did you hear what the message was?"

"Sorry, no, they just called out your name."

"Like the boy said, we'll have to ask around!" Len grinned.

Carol smiled and squeezed his hand. He threaded a path toward the tables in the rear of the Soda Shack. "It's usually quieter back there."

Carol peered hopefully through the people, but couldn't see any available tables for two.

"Did you get your message?" shouted David, practically into Carol's ear. He held Elisha with her back toward him in a complex arrangement of intertwined arms.

"No one seems to know who answered the phone." Carol looked puzzled while the other couple circled Len and her with the elaborate step and the slow deliberation of a primitive rite.

"Ask Mrs. Cooper," suggested Elisha. And she ducked into a series of solo spins that turned her long white hair into a dangerous whip.

Len and Carol leaped off the dance floor.

"That's some step!" he teased after they had caught their breath.

"Over here! Hey, Len! Carol!" shouted Mrs. R. "We've saved you two seats!"

"Leonard Whitkins!" called her redheaded daughter,

standing on a chair and waving her arms.

"Author! Author!" the voice of Val's new football player boyfriend boomed over all the other noises: the rock music, the deep fat sizzle, the clunking of glasses, the rattle of dishes, the vociferous conversations.

Michael, Dana, and Jordan, three juniors who had played students in *Extracurricular,* bounced up and down trying to attract attention to Mrs. R.'s table near the back wall.

"I think we better get over there before they go through the floor."

"Or the ceiling," agreed Carol as they charted their course through the tables, chairs, and customers.

"Okay, we're coming!" Len shouted. But only after they removed their jackets and were seated, did the general commotion settle down to a dull roar.

Val greeted them, "We were waiting and waiting and . . ."

"You have no idea how difficult it's been to hold these seats," her boyfriend interrupted.

"If your mother hadn't phoned we would have . . ."

Carol interrupted, "Is that the message everyone keeps mentioning?"

". . . called out the National Guard or something! Where have you been?" Val confronted Carol, completely ignoring her friend's question about the telephone call.

"We stopped to look at the sky," Len answered Val for her.

From the next table where she sat with Pat, four other costume girls and two stage crew boys, Mrs. Cooper asked, "Is that what they call it, now?"

Len replied, "I have no idea what you're talking about!" And he slipped his arm around Carol's shoulders.

Carol felt her face break into the same silly grin she had tried to hide earlier in the evening. She smiled at

Mrs. Cooper, the crew, the other cast members, Val's boyfriend, and Mrs. R. Carol was delighted to see each of them look back at her with understanding. She knew, as she leaned against Len's arm, that his casual gesture made a statement as clear as any announcement.

"Ain't love grand," stated Jordan, enthusiastically placing his arm around Dana.

"I hate to be a killjoy, Carol," said Mrs. R. "But it's almost time for you to be starting home."

The glasses of melting ice cubes and the greasy dishes on both tables proved Val's complaint about their late arrival. But Carol had no idea of what time it was. She knew that she felt wide awake and full of energy in spite of last night's late rehearsal and tonight's performance.

Before Carol could respond, Pat protested, "But she hasn't even had anything to eat yet!"

"I don't think she feels hungry," Dana observed with a silly grin that mirrored Carol's.

"If you want to eat something, I can drive you home afterwards," offered Mrs. R. "It just seems like a good night for a walk," she added with exaggerated casualness.

"Wait a minute," interrupted Len, "what's all this about Carol's going home." He addressed her directly, "Aren't your parents supposed to be coming?"

"Didn't anyone tell you about their phone call?" interjected Mrs. Cooper.

"Everyone's told me about that phone call, but nobody seems to know what the message was!" Carol's exasperation jerked her body upright away from Len's arm.

"Oh, I'm afraid that's my fault," said Mrs. R. "I wasn't paying close enough attention. I thought Val must have told you about it! Please, forgive me."

"Gladly, if you'll tell what the caller said!"

"Well, Marcy took the message."

"No, I didn't; it was Lou, right after you dropped the french fries."

"This is like a soap opera," Len said with frustration.

"Well, where's Lou?" asked Marcy.

"Come on!" Len threw his hands toward the ceiling. "The suspense is killing me."

There was another pause while everyone laughed. Finally Val's boyfriend blurted out, "Carol's parents aren't coming! And she's supposed to be home before midnight!"

"Turning into a pumpkin?" quipped Michael. "It's almost eleven-thirty now."

"The costume department has several pairs of glass slippers," offered one of the Home Ec. majors.

"They must be left over from the children's theatre."

"We should start that up again."

The conversation drifted away from Carol's curfew.

"At least they've stopped talking about that telephone call," Len whispered.

"They're right, though, I'll have to leave soon. It really isn't fair, no one else has to go so early."

"A lot of kids leave around midnight." He squeezed her shoulders. "Are you feeling a sudden desire for cheese or pie shells?"

"No, but if I had a glass slipper, I might be tempted to use it violently on the next Cinderella joker."

"You mean we have the wrong fairy tale; you're really going to turn into," Len paused and pitched his voice to a loud stage whisper, "a werewolf!"

"A werewolf!" squealed one of the costume girls letting her eyes go round with mock fear.

"Len, you better get Carol out of here before Marcy faints!" warned Mark, one of the stage crew members.

"Marcy, we're going to have to put you on the stage

in the spring!" Len threatened while he and Carol stood up and gathered their outdoor clothing.

"I trust you'll be able to enter her heart and hold off the evil curse," teased Michael.

Len struck his chest with his right fist, "I'm willing to take the chance for the sake of West Egelton Senior High!"

"Goodnight, everyone!" Carol waved with one hand, while she tugged on Len's arm with the other. "Say goodnight, Len."

"Goodnight, Len," he grinned.

"Have a nice walk home."

"Goodbye! Congratulations on a great show!"

"Goodnight."

"Don't do anything we wouldn't do!"

By the time they reached the street groups of students blocked the sidewalk.

"You see, you're not the only one!" Len took her arm. They quickly walked away from the crowded main street.

"But I want to spend the whole night celebrating!" She persisted as they passed quiet private homes illuminated by the glow of television screens.

"How about all day tomorrow?" he suggested, guiding her around the icy patches on the snow-topped street.

"We have a brunch date." Carol let herself grin triumphantly. She was alone with Len. And he was holding her hand.

"And don't think for a minute that I'm going to let you get out of it!" Suddenly Len released her hand. "Here's the car." Len took the keys out of his pocket and opened the door. "It feels funny to have to ask, but where do you live?"

"Over there!" She pointed to a two-story wood and brick house half a block from Len's parking spot.

"Would you mind very much if we walked?" he asked ignoring her laughter. "It's such a nice night."

"Only because it's you." She attempted to match his tone of superior dignity. "I wouldn't consider it with anyone else." And she knew she meant it.

chapter
★.★ 12 ★.★

"Well, here it is, kid, your portfolio of office!" Len pulled a heavy cardboard folder from the bookshelf in Mr. Carter's office and handed it to Carol.

She placed it on the desk and loosened the string to release the top flap. "What is all this stuff? It looks like a portable stationery store."

"You'll have to ask Elisha; it's been all I could do to sort out David's junk from the presidential file. I think he used it as a spare locker."

"Congratulations, President Whitkins, Vice-President Clark." Mr. Carter crossed the office to his desk. "I think the Drama Club voted very wisely."

"Especially since we ran unopposed," quipped Len.

"This a study break?"

"Sort of; you gave us passes to work on plans for the spring play." Len pointed at the presigned pass book.

"I did?" Mr. Carter asked, settling into his chair. "Did I also suggest that you should do it in my office?"

"Only if you were out!" replied the Drama Club's new president.

"Well, I seem to be in at the moment."

"Nancy's setting up the files for this term's classes," Carol pointed out as an excuse.

"The reception area looks like an explosion in a confetti factory!"

"Do you two think I like those pink, green, yellow, orange, blue, and white cards?"

"Doesn't everybody?"

"We'll work in the auditorium," stated Carol, closing the file envelope and gathering her books.

"It's locked."

"All right, we'll sit on the stone benches in the lobby." Len's tone lost its lightness.

"You'd better take an extra set of passes. It would be embarrassing to bail the Drama Club officers out of the detention room."

"That's okay," grinned Len. "I've learned to keep an extra set in my wallet." He held the door open for Carol.

"See you later, Mr. C."

"I expect some solid suggestions from this collaboration."

"We'll do our best," Carol assured him.

Neither Nancy nor her two assistants lifted their eyes from their filing when Len and Carol passed through the reception cubical.

"It feels like a final exam's being given in there," commented Carol when they had closed the door to the hall behind them.

"Fortunately, it only happens for two days each year."

The empty hall echoed slightly. Len set a fast pace for the nearby lobby. They relaxed on a low marble bench near the glass wall that separated the lobby from the snowbound sculpture garden.

"You look beautiful in this light; who'd guess you're an old lady of sixteen."

Carol laughed, "Len, can't you ever just give a plain compliment?"

"That's the secret of my charm; it drives the women wild!"

His eyes met hers. They leaned toward each other across the barrier of books and papers. Before they could touch, the sound of footsteps catapulted both their bodies to rigidly upright positions.

"A little cool for the Honor's Garden," stated Mr. Brockton apparently unaware of what he had interrupted.

"But it's still very beautiful," responded Carol. "Mr. Brockton, do you know Len Whitkins?"

"Yes, indeed, Len was in my freshman honor's mathematics just like you are now."

"It's funny, you know, I was afraid when I had to take math; but I was so busy last term, I forgot my fear of numbers!"

The teacher smiled slightly, "Of course, I'll undoubtedly lose you to the theatre as well. I understand congratulations are in order."

"Thank you, Mr. Brockton." Carol was always amazed at how much her homeroom teacher seemed to know about each of his students.

"You're most welcome, Carol. I look forward to seeing you on the stage in the spring." He nodded and without looking back walked briskly across the lobby toward the administrative offices.

Len reached for Carol's hand. Their eyes locked again.

"Carry on with whatever it was that you were doing." Mr. Brockton's voice echoed between the brick and the glass walls.

Carol felt her laughter effervesce like bubbles in bottled water. She grasped at Len's hand to anchor her through the bout of silliness.

It was contagious. The two of them dissolved in laughter. Each time their eyes met the merriment increased. Then, unexpectedly, all at once it stopped.

Carol found she was still holding Len's hand. She felt him pull her toward him.

"Sounds like some party!"

"Warming up for Saturday night?"

Carol turned to see Elisha and David rounding the corner of the auditorium.

"Mr. C. said we'd find you two here!" David stopped his girlfriend before they reached the bench by the windows. "But it looks like you're busy."

"No, wait a minute." Carol found herself standing. She was being responsible in spite of her desire to be alone with Len. "Elisha, what is all the stuff in here?"

The other girl approached the bench. She looked at the red cardboard folder as if she had never seen it before. "What's that?"

"The Drama Club Vice-Presidential portfolio!" exclaimed Carol with impatience.

"Oh, that!" pronounced Elisha. "I never used it. Last year's secretary insisted on making one up for each new officer. But I just let David do all the work." She hung on his arm like an overripe peach on its branch.

"Don't go planting any ideas in Carol's head!" Len waved his arms emphatically as if to push the two blonds away.

"Carol's much too sensible to take ideas from Elisha," teased David, squeezing the ex-vice-president.

Elisha wiggled free from her tormentor. "How's your mother, Len?"

"Much better, thanks,"

"She's walking with a cane now," added Carol. "Dad and I are really glad to have her home."

"It must be almost a month," calculated David.

"She sure has improved the condition of your wardrobe!" Elisha stared at Len's green flannel shirt.

"No, that's Carol's work. She's teaching me how to sew." He smiled at Carol.

"That's the idea," Elisha nodded approvingly. "Train

them while they're young and impressionable."

"David, do something!" Len demanded.

"What do you suggest?"

"She's bigger than I am, I don't dare suggest anything!"

Elisha ignored the two boys. "That's a great outfit. I couldn't wear anything like it, but on you it's marvelous. It brings out your coloring. And it also gives you a suggestion of authority as if you're truly sure of yourself."

Carol felt a blush creep over her cheeks. She forced her nervous hands to rest against the soft wool of the flared red and navy striped skirt. "Thanks, Elisha. During vacation my parents took me to New York City for a day's shopping. It was a sort of combination of Christmas and birthday gifts."

"Isn't your birthday on Saturday?" asked David.

"No, it was the day before yesterday."

"But the party's on Saturday!" he exclaimed with a big smile.

Carol smiled back, "You're both coming aren't you?"

"Sure, with bells on!"

Elisha continued speaking as if the topic had not changed. "It's amazing that we both look good in red, but the effect's totally different."

Carol knew Elisha was comparing her own scarlet blouse with the terra-cotta shirt that matched the pinstripes in Carol's skirt.

"There's a great new store in town, Discount Dress Designs, we could go there together sometime."

"Sure, that's where I bought the dress I wore..." Carol stopped herself before she mentioned the date with David. "I've been there. It's great. You're absolutely right."

"I hate to interrupt the fashion news," Len looked like a boy scout helping an old lady into a mud puddle. "But we have work to do before the bell rings."

"We came by to answer your questions regarding your new responsibilities," David took Elisha's arm. "But as there are five months before you'll be totally on your own, I suppose we can leave you to settle into your new office." His sweeping hand gestured to imply the lobby had become Len's and Carol's private space.

"See you Saturday," Elisha called over her shoulder as David led her back toward the drama office.

"If not before," answered Carol.

"I gather you may no longer want to do a musical," Len teased.

"She's really not that bad when you get to know her."

"And when you're out of the running for David."

"Am I out of the running? I know I look better now than I did last term. And I feel better about myself, too."

"That's true; you've grown up." Len looked at Carol in mock distress. "At least I thought you had, but if you're still chasing after David you may still have a bit of learning to do."

"Did I say I was chasing after David?" she teased him back. Fluttering her eyelashes she sighed, "I just don't think it's good to be called out of the running."

"Shall I prove it's true?" Len stepped close to Carol and grasped her wrists.

"Prove what? That I'm out of the running or that it's good that I'm out of the running?" She pretended to be indifferent to Len's nearness. However, inside Carol felt her heart dance to a quicker beat as Len puller her toward him again.

The sound of approaching footsteps interrupted their conversation.

139

Len dropped Carol's right arm. He spun around and leaned hard on the spring release of the glass door marked Honor Students Only!

"Come on," he pulled her by the left wrist, "we're both qualified."

"Don't you think honor students are supposed to be smart enough to stay in out of the snow?" she asked as he lead her through the untrod whiteness to a spot behind a snowdrift covering a large sculpture. "I bet you take all your girls here."

"No, only the one that's first in the running!" Len wrapped his arms around Carol as she tilted her face up to his.

The icy wetness in her shoes, the cold air, and their responsibilities all seemed to vanish. Then the bell rang!